SEASON OUT OF TIME

By: Timothy D. Wise

Published by: Emporium Press
*The Publishing Division of Professor Theophilus' Emporium
of Imagination, Inc.*
Magnolia, Arkansas

Season Out of Time. Copyright 2005
by Professor Theophilus' Emporium of Imagination, Inc.
Timothy D. Wise, President

Published by:
EMPORIUM PRESS
The Publishing Division of Professor Theophilus' Emporium
of Imagination, Inc.
Magnolia, Arkansas

Cover Design by: Timothy D. Wise

Library of Congress Control Number: 2005903687

First Edition
ISBN: 0972554947

DEDICATION:

To Ms. Gina Gilreath and her junior high English class at Parker's Chapel.

ACKNOWLEDGEMENTS

I want to express my appreciation to Ms. Gina Gilreath-Loony and her junior high English class and to Mrs. Pat Gilreath for their enthusiastic support of this book when it was only an unpublished manuscript. Their encouragement and the publicity it generated helped to drive the creation of Emporium Press as well as this book.

Naturally I want to thank my family for their support of my work. My Mom has seen this story in all its many forms. I thank my Uncle Dan and Aunt Rose and my cousins Sandy, Warren, and Gina who used to take my family and me to see the mysterious Brown Mountain lights in North Carolina.

Thanks to Stephen Spielberg and George Lucas for bringing us *Close Encounters of the Third Kind* and *Star Wars* back in 1977 and to Sony Entertainment for allowing my references to *Close Encounters* in *Season*. The title, though not an exact quote, was inspired by a line from the song "Seasons in the Sun," written by Jacques Brel and Rod McKuen and performed by Terry Jacks.

PROLOGUE

It was June 4, 1977. My birthday. I had just turned twelve, and I felt like an Egyptian king in a tomb full of gold-plated wonders. My flying model rocket, my glue-together model of the bionic man, my tape recorder, and my comic books were arranged on the coffee table in front of me like gifts on an altar. I was eating some of my birthday cake, drinking A&W Root Beer from a cold glass bottle, and watching television. Life was pretty much perfect.

The phone rang. I picked it up and had barely said "hello" when someone started jabbering away in one big run-on sentence.

"Jim you've got to come down to Miracle Mountain Park there was a UFO and something came out of it and crashed on Ghost Mountain and the police are all going up there and you've got to come see it!"

"What?"

Another ramble of words crowded their way through the receiver. I halfway expected the top of phone to blow off.

Somewhere in the middle of that rush of words, I had recognized the voice. It was Jaime Mitchell. I had just met Jaime a little over a week ago, but she had quickly become one of my best friends. She had just been at my house for a birthday party so I wasn't that surprised to hear from her again.

"What did you just say?"

"There was a UFO."

"I heard that part. Where did you say you were?"

"Miracle Mountain Park!"

Miracle Mountain was an amusement park located on the edge of our town. I could hear the roar of the crowd and the people screaming on the roller coaster.

"What are you doing there?" I asked. I suddenly went from thinking life was perfect to being envious.

"I ran away from home."

That wasn't what I'd expected to hear.

"What?"

"I can't live with my mom anymore, Jim. She's going crazy. She found out I went to your birthday party without her permission . . ."

"I thought you said she let you come."

"I lied," she admitted. "I'm still grounded."

"Well, no wonder she got mad."

"She didn't just get mad. She went crazy. She slapped me and started crying and cussing. It scared me. I've never seen her like that. That's why I'm running away."

"Where are you going to sleep tonight?" I asked her. None of this made any sense.

""I don't know," she said. I thought she was going to cry. Then she changed the subject.

"Jim, there really was a UFO; a big one."

"Is this real or are you playing *Close Encounters*?" My mom had just taken all of us to see *Close Encounters of the Third Kind* as part of the birthday festivities.

"Real! I'm not playing! It was over Ghost Mountain. Then a helicopter came out of it and crashed over there close to where the wax museum is."

"A helicopter came out of a UFO?" I'm sure I sounded pretty smart alecky.

"Stop being a butt!" Jaime told me. "You've got to come see!"

"My parents went to the grocery store," I told her. "I'll get them to take me when they get back."

"You've got to come *now*!" she insisted. "By the time your parents get home, they prob'ly won't let people through. They'll have the army up there like they did on *Close Encounters*."

"If I come now I'll get in trouble," I said.

"Chicken!"

"I'm not a chicken. I'll come when they get back."

"I'm sorry I called you a chicken," Jaime said. "You're my only real friend. I just want you to come. I don't want to go up there by myself."

"I'll come when my folks get home," I told her. "I promise."

"Okay."

I hung up and waited, on pins and needles, for my parents to get home. When they finally did come home, I could tell something was wrong. I could tell my mom had been crying and Dad looked like he was about to.

"Jim," Dad said. "Son, we've got something to tell you."

"What?"

"It's Jaime. She's . . . she's gone, son."

"She ran away?"

I nearly laughed to myself. I already knew that.

"She died."

That stopped me cold.

"She's dead?" I felt myself starting to tear up. "How did it happen?"

"She was on her bike. Somebody hit her."

* * *

MIRACLE SPRING, AR—12-year-old Jaime Mitchell was struck and killed by a police car involved in a high-speed chase on Holland Ridge. The accident occurred Saturday night following an alleged UFO sighting and an unexplained helicopter crash. Sheriff's Deputy Billy Neeson is under investigation for allegedly driving under the influence of alcohol. Neeson is recovering from injuries sustained in the crash. Also killed in the crash were Deputy Will Beavers and an unidentified individual who was fleeing from the police on a motorcycle.

I smoothed the article out and set it on the table beside the rest of the evidence. I punched the "record" and "play" buttons on my tape recorder.

"June 12, 1977. Jim Koslow reporting. I've been investigating the cause of Jaime's death for over a week now. I know she wasn't just killed by a drunk driver. There's more to it than that. I believe there were aliens involved. Today I found the evidence to prove it. I had to climb down into the valley where Jaime died. I had to crawl down clay cliffs by hanging onto roots. I had to crawl through brush and sticker briars."

My legs were perforated with angry red scratches. I should not have worn shorts.

"It was tough, but it was worth it. I finally found the evidence I was looking for."

I held it up into the light. Rainbow colors played across the mirrored surface.

"It's a silver disk about . . ." I stopped and held it up to a ruler. ". . . Just under five inches in diameter. There's writing on one side. CD-RW. The other side is silver, and there's a hole in the middle. It looks kind of like a record, but it's smooth. There aren't any grooves. I don't know what it is, but I'm going to find out. If it takes the rest of my life, I swear I'll find out what really happened to Jaime."

I punched the stop button. I carefully wrapped the disk in aluminum foil and tucked it into a shoe box.

Chapter 1: Ghosts of the Past, Shades of the Future

"That was a good presentation," Dr. Tarkington told me as we came out of the elevator. "Kept the students involved."

Tarkington was a tall, bearded man in his fifties. His long hair was slicked back from his forehead, and it looked wet from the shower. He was wearing a Hawaiian print shirt and khakis.

"When will the committee make its decision?" I asked.

"Give it about a week," he said as we walked down the hall toward his office.

"Hey, Tark," a tall blonde said as she passed us. "How's it going?"

"Hey, Lindsey," Tarkington answered, smiling.

"They call you Tark?" I asked.

"Some of them do," Tarkington said. He laughed. "So, James, what do you think about our school? They do call you James?"

"Since I started college," I told him. "They called me *Jim* before that."

"So what do you think?" he asked as he pulled out his keys and unlocked the door of his office. The door was varnished wood with a transom over the top. Tarkington had cartoons taped to his door beside his class schedule. Most of the cartoons were of aliens—either the Martian from Bugs Bunny or the gray, big-eyed variety.

"It's nice," I said. "Beautiful campus."

"Kind of out of the way," Tarkington said. "That's the complaint we sometimes get from people who like crowded streets and traffic jams. So what about you? Does that bother you?"

He opened the door, and we stepped into the office.

"I grew up here," I told him, "and after being in Houston for a while, I could use a little peace and quiet."

He grunted agreement. I looked around at his office. He had a big movie poster from *Close Encounters of the Third Kind* framed and placed on one wall. The poster showed a man and woman running down a highway toward a flat-topped mountain. It stirred up memories of the summer of 1977, the summer everything had changed.

The shelves were overflowing with books and stacks of paper. He had alien souvenirs everywhere. There were alien saltshakers, a road sign pointing to Roswell, New Mexico where a UFO crash was supposed to have taken place, alien statuettes and rubber masks. Outside the window, stately oak trees were clothed in the bright greens of late spring. Students walked between columned buildings, sat on benches around a pond that would have been at home in a painting, lay on picnic blankets.

"Come on in," Tarkington said. "Sit down."

"This is quite a place you've got here," I said. "Why all the aliens?"

Tarkington laughed.

"The students give them to me," he said. "They go places and bring them back."

"But why aliens?" I asked.

"It's my research," he said. "I've done some work with SETI. You know about that, right?"

"The Search for Extraterrestrial Intelligence," I said. "The antennas and all."

"Right," he said. "Right. Mostly, though, I spend a lot of time researching the phenomena around Ghost Mountain. You know, the lights."

"I grew up here," I told him. "My brothers and I used to ride our bikes out to look at them."

"There are places like that all over the country," Tarkington said. "You've got the Marfa Lights in Texas, the Brown Mountain Lights up near Ashville, North Carolina—the list goes on."

"And they date back to ancient times," I said.

"Yeah," he said. "From back before the white man ever came to this part of the world. The Indians stayed clear of Ghost Mountain because of those lights. They thought the place was sacred." His face darkened. "Maybe I should have listened to them."

"Don't some people claim to see ghostly figures?" I asked.

"Yeah," he said. "Native Americans in animal skins. Women in long dresses and bonnets. They're usually there only for a few seconds, but some people claim to have had conversations with them. Nobody's ever been able to prove it. Hard thing to prove, I guess."

"When did the government buy the mountain?" I asked.

"About twenty years ago," he said. "It's been off limits to the public since then."

"A lot of people think that has something to do with the lights," I said. "What do you think?"

"Who knows why the government does anything?" he said. That wasn't really an answer.

"But they let you in to do your studies?"

"Yeah. They let me in." He sighed. "Anyway, back to the job interview. So you grew up here, but went to college somewhere else?"

"I got a scholarship to another school," I told him. "And after growing up here, I was ready to get out and see what the rest of the world was like. I guess I never realized how special this place was."

Dr. Tarkington shuffled the file folders on his desk.

"And you've had your doctorate in physics for the past five years?"

"Yes."

"And you've been working for NASA in Houston all during that time."

"Mostly, yes. I do some independent consulting work too."

"I see. So tell me, Dr. James Koslow: Why would you want to leave your work at NASA to come here?"

"I'll keep up my consulting work," I told him, "but I've been running nonstop for nearly ten years. I'd like to slow the pace down a bit, maybe do some writing."

"And teaching?" Tarkington said. "That's an important part of the job here. You're a trained scientist. Are you sure you want to teach physical science to a bunch of unruly freshmen who give you nicknames behind your back and put aliens on your door?"

"I decided to become a scientist because of my sixth grade science teacher," I told him. "He opened up a whole new world to me."

"And you think you'd like to try to do that for the students here?"

"Yes."

"Well," he said. "You'll certainly have your work cut out for you. This isn't a big city university, Dr. Koslow, and our students aren't generally what you'd find on the campuses of Ivy League schools."

"I know this school's reputation," I told him. "Your graduates have done some pretty impressive things. They've started companies, written books . . ."

"Yeah," he said. "That's true. I see you did your homework." Tarkington rose to his feet. "So tell me about your work at NASA. Was it exciting?"

"The idea of working there was exciting," I told him. "But it wasn't like every day was filled with great discoveries."

"Not quite the way you pictured it as a boy, eh?" he asked.

"Not quite," I told him. "I do value the time I spent there though."

"Sure," he said. "Sure. It's just that things don't always turn out the way you expect. Be careful what you wish for, James. The world's full of monkey paws."

"Monkey paws?" I asked him. It seemed like a strange thing to say.

"Yeah," he said. "It's an old short story by Somerset Maughm. I hope they're still teaching that in English class. It's valuable stuff."

"What happens in the story?" I asked.

"This explorer's visiting his friend in England," Tarkington said. "He's been all over the world. You know, to Africa, India, Tibet. In one of those places a holy man gave him this shriveled monkey's paw. It has the power to make wishes come true, but it's dangerous. Anyway, the explorer leaves it with his friend. His friend wishes for ten thousand pounds. The next day his son dies in an industrial accident and the company gives him ten thousand pounds from his son's insurance policy. It goes downhill from there. Creepy, huh?"

"Yeah," I said. I noticed Tarkington had a newspaper clipping cut out and sitting on his desk. He kept glancing at it during out discussion. At the top of the clipping was a headline, "Student Dies." Beneath it was a grainy, black and white photograph of a young man.

"What happened to the guy in the clipping?" I asked.

"What?" Tarkington said.

"The clipping on your desk," I said. "You keep looking at it."

He raised his elbows from his desk and looked around. He picked up the newspaper clipping and sighed.

"This boy was my student worker," he said. "A great kid. His name was Keith Anderson."

"What happened to him?" I asked again.

"He died in an accident on one of my expeditions," Tarkington said. He looked down, avoiding my gaze. "He—uh—fell out of a helicopter."

"That's terrible," I said. "When did it happen?"

"Back in April," he said. "About six weeks ago."

"I'm sorry," I said.

He nodded. Then he rose to his feet and extended a hand.

"Thank you for coming, James. I'll let you know as soon as the committee makes its decision." He smiled though his eyes were still sad. "I think they were impressed with your presentation."

The sun was settling low in the sky when I drove through the main gate that separated the campus of Green Mountain University from the rest of the community. It was, in ways, like passing through a time portal. The campus, with its columned buildings, oaks, and bell tower, seemed sacred and set apart from the surrounding world. Miracle Springs was a tourist town built around a chain of mountain lakes. It was a place of resort hotels, miniature golf courses and go-cart tracks for children and casinos and bars for adults.

I had grown up there, like I had told Dr. Tarkington, and had moved away after high school, but there was more to the story than just getting a scholarship. I had loved Miracle Springs the whole time I was growing up, but Jaime's death had changed everything. It had dropped, like a dark cloud, over everything that had made the town magical, special, and fun. The pain was bearable now, and I thought it might be safe to return.

The main road into town skirted the edge of a large mountain lake. Hotels and condos had sprung up along the lake's pristine shores, but the forests along the hillside were still intact. Jet skis cut their mosquito paths along the gleaming skin of the lake's chilly waters. The sailboats looked like white moth wings.

On the opposite shore of the lake, I could see a vacant lot where Miracle Mountain Park had once stood. I remembered roller coaster tracks and a chairlift that went out over the lake. Off to my left I could see the grim shape of Ghost Mountain brooding over the town like a dark spirit.

A gate with armed guards blocked the only road that led up onto the mountain. The story was that the place served as a type of survival training facility, but I still wondered about the purpose of the giant radio transmitter that stood at the apex of the tallest peak.

I drove down Main Street, taking in every change. A new Tex-Mex restaurant had just sprung up and the old drive-in theater was now a parking lot. I turned off onto a side street and drove past the middle school where I'd spent my fifth and sixth grades. The old playground still resonated with the imaginary aura our youthful imaginations had given it. The area beneath those pine trees had been a haunted forest, an island filled with dinosaurs, dozens of alien planets . . .

After about five minutes of driving, I turned by the E-Z Stop, and drove up the winding mountain road behind it. This was the road I had lived on. Green River wound beneath the trees beside the road. I remembered my dad taking my brothers and me down that river in an orange rubber raft when I was in middle school. I passed a house where Leonard Delaney, my sixth grade science teacher, had once lived. The roof was falling in. I felt a stab of sadness. I had wished many times that I could tell him about getting a doctorate in physics and working for NASA. He would have been thrilled. A droplet hit my windshield. A light rain was starting to fall.

Finally I turned into a long driveway. Gravel cracked beneath my tires as I rolled up to my parent's two-story house at the foot of the mountain. My parents were waiting at the door when I drove up. I didn't even have to knock.

"How was the interview?" they both asked, clearly thrilled by the prospect of having me back in the area after so long.

"Fine," I told them, "but I won't know anything until the committee has had a chance to meet."

After hugging them and telling them about my life in Houston, I lugged my suitcase upstairs to the second bedroom on the left. My mom followed me.

There were still two twin beds in the room. I could still picture my brother Jason lying there moaning and scratching himself because he didn't want to get up for school. I remembered singing songs about him and generally aggravating him on those mornings. I laughed to myself and felt a little bit guilty at the same time. The carpet was the same. The shape of the room was the same. Everything else had changed. The old toys were all packed away. The posters--both the superhero and monster posters of the earlier years and the rock star and Heather Thomas posters of later years--were gone. The walls were bare. The room was neat and clean like a hotel room. I looked out the window. Rain poured down on the empty yard outside.

"I just got through painting the walls in here," Mom said.

"It looks nice," I said. It did. But it didn't look anything at all like the room I had remembered. Every trace of me was long gone.

"We just got some of our old home movies transferred to DVD," my dad said. He was standing in the door. "We can watch them later if you want to." We used to watch the old 8mm home movies a lot on holidays—at least until our 1950s model projector had given up the ghost.

"Sounds good," I told Dad. "I've missed them."

"Do you want some coffee?" Mom asked. "I've got chocolate macadamia nut." She stopped. "Have you even had supper yet?"

"I ate at the college," I said. "The coffee sounds good, though."

We walked back downstairs to the den. Mom went into the kitchen and started the coffee brewing. I followed her in. Dad was behind me. I smiled as I saw the cake sitting on the table. I wasn't really surprised.

"Happy birthday, Jim," Mom said.

They handed me a present, and I unwrapped it. It was a DVD of a movie, *Close Encounters of the Third Kind*.

"I haven't seen this in years," I said. I thought of the poster on Tarkington's wall and of the bittersweet memories it brought back. Jaime and I had watched the movie together just before the accident that took her life. I had not been able to watch it since then. I wondered if my parents knew that. I also wondered if enough time had passed that I could watch the movie and enjoy it.

"Do you want your cake now," Mom asked, "or do you want to wait on the coffee?"

"I can wait," I said. "For chocolate macadamia nut, anyway."

Mom made coffee while Dad seated himself at the table.

"Dr. Tarkington was telling me about an accident," I said. "One of his students was killed."

"About six weeks ago," Dad said. "That was a strange deal."

"Why strange?"

"They were missing for nearly a week," Dad said. "It turned out the Air Force had been holding them. They had already prepared that boy for burial by the time anybody knew he was dead."

"That *is* strange," I said.

"Have you talked to Larry yet?" Mom asked. Larry Christopher was a friend of mine.

"No," I said. "I just got here."

I walked over to the basement, opened the door, and peered down into darkness. The basement had been a childhood hideout. The damp, earthy smell made me sentimental.

After a time of eating cake, drinking coffee, and waxing nostalgic, my parents and I moved into the den to watch home movies. The movies had been filmed on a box camera before the days when home movies had sound. Faded images from the fifties--my dad's red and white Oldsmobile convertible, a high school party at the lake, a trip to Black Canyon in Colorado, and younger-looking ghosts of my grandparents flashed across the screen. The guys at the video production place had added a musical sound track. An instrumental version of "Run for the

Roses" played in the background. *They were younger than I am*, I thought.

My brothers and I entered the drama in the mid-1960s. I was born in '65. Jason came along a year later and Barry, the caboose, entered the world in December of '69. On the video I saw Barry toddling around in yellow double-knit pants, white baby shoes, and a shirt with something spilled on it. Jason, my middle brother, was missing his two front teeth in one of the pictures. Mine had just grown back and looked too big for my mouth. In those flickering moments, my parents and I relived several Christmases, summer vacation trips, birthday parties, graduations . . .

Sometimes I wish I could go back and relive those times," Mom said.

I had no idea how prophetic her statement would turn out to be.

Suddenly we were older. I had just turned twelve. The day, in early June, was bright with the shining green of late spring. Jason, ten, was wearing a Farrah Fawcett tee shirt. My mom had set up a couple of picnic tables in the back yard. I could see her shadow holding the camera. My dad, his hair still black, was tending to some steaks on the grill.

The camera panned around the back yard. Barry, six, was playing with Cindy, our Boston Terrier. The badminton net was set up. Jason had picked up a racket and was playing on one side of the net along with Larry Christopher. Larry looked so thin, and he looked so much happier than he had during most of his childhood. I was playing on the other side of the net swinging a racket. Next to me was a girl almost my age, almost twelve. She was wearing bellbottoms, sandals, and a white shirt with puffed sleeves, and, like Larry, she looked happy.

"Jaime," I whispered.

It was Jaime Mitchell--only hours before she had died.

"Poor little Jaime," my mom said. "I'll never forget coming home and telling you about her that night—on your birthday."

No, I thought. *I'll never forget it either.*

"We almost didn't tell you," Dad said. "We thought about waiting until the next day."

"She's in a better place," Mom said. This was a quiet expression of a long-held faith.

"Pretty much ended life for her mama, though," Dad said.

"I'm afraid Jaime's mother was just sorry anyway," Mom said. "Last I heard, she and her live-in boyfriend had been arrested for selling dope. No telling what Jaime would have gone through if she had lived."

"I always felt like the tragedy did it to her," Dad said. "I don't think she would ever have done anything like that otherwise. She just went a little bit crazy after losing Jaime."

"You just liked the way she looked," Mom said.

"She looked nice," Dad shrugged. Then he changed the subject. "There's Mr. Delaney. I hadn't thought about him in years."

An older man with a full head of gray hair and wire-rimmed glasses appeared on the screen. He was laughing with my parents about something. Leonard Delaney. It was his house I had passed earlier.

"He didn't live long after that either," my Mom said.

"No," I said. "He didn't."

"I'm glad I took those pictures that day," Mom said. Mr. Delaney had died of a heart attack about six months after my twelfth birthday. He had retired from teaching in early June only to die the following November. His wife had died of cancer two years before, and he didn't have any children. I remember my mom saying that he had died of loneliness.

This was starting to get depressing. It was as if this short video segment had captured the last hours of my childhood. The deaths of my friend and my teacher had kicked me too soon into a world of mortality and death. That was the summer my innocence—my sense of immortality—had ended.

The camera panned along the picnic table past my dad and past Mr. Delaney to a man in a tee shirt and bellbottoms. He quickly turned away from the camera, but I was sure I had seen him before.

"Who was that?" I asked.

"One of Mr. Delaney's former students," Mom said. "He was staying in town for a few days."

"I think I remember him," I said. "I met him at school. Then later on he went through the wax museum with Jaime, Larry, and me. He just happened to be driving along that day we got caught in the rain. I can't believe I'd forgotten him. I think his name was James too."

"You kids talked him into going to *Close Encounters* with you too," Mom said.

"I remember him, now," I said. "I guess I forgot about him after Jaime's accident. It's like I blocked out everything that happened during those few weeks."

"Do you remember what he looked like?" Mom asked.

"Yes," I said. "The best I remember, he looked kind of like me—the way I look now. Weird. It's probably my memory playing tricks on me."

Somehow I knew that the stranger's appearance in my life was more than coincidence. Something else was starting to tug at my subconscious too.

All of the children in the movie gathered around as Mr. Delaney connected the wires from the battery of my dad's ride-on lawn mower to a rocket on a launch pad. The camera panned to me punching a button and swung up through the evening sky until it found a dark shape shooting upwards, stopping, and falling to earth on a parachute. Mr. Delaney, my sixth grade science teacher. He had come over that night to give me his model rocket and launcher. Since he had retired, he said, he wouldn't be needing them anymore. That seemed kind of sad.

The scene changed again. Everyone onscreen was seated around the table. Dad's image silently asked Mr. Delaney's reflection to return a silent prayer of thanksgiving and the steak, rolls, and potato salad were passed around. The camera panned around the table. James, the stranger, carefully avoided the camera.

"Camera shy," Mom said.

Finally the camera stopped on Jaime. She looked into the lens, crossed her eyes, and laughed. That was the last scene.

"Goodbye, Jaime." I thought it rather than saying it.

The picture faded to scratches and bands of color and finally vanished altogether. I expected to hear the film pulling loose from the reel and slapping against it as it spun around. Those sounds, like the images on the tape, were things of the past.

I sat in the den and talked with my parents for hours. The conversation reached a lull.

"It's nearly midnight," my dad said after a long moment of silence. "I know you've had a long day."

"I guess we better get ready for bed," Mom said.

"I think I'll stay down here a little while longer," I said. "Get used to being home again."

"I've got a few dishes to wash," Mom said. She went over to the sink.

I walked over to the kitchen window, looked out at the storm.

A bolt of lightning flash-photographed the mountains. A clap of thunder exploded like an artillery burst through the dark gulf overhead. I closed my eyes and felt the universe shiver around me. Suddenly I knew what I had been trying to remember. A chill went through my body as I saw it playing out like a surreal home movie in front of me.

Jaime was dead, and I knew the aliens had had something to do with it. This was the darkest time of my life. The joy and innocence of my former childhood had been ripped from me. Jaime's death had been caused by a police car pursuing a strange man on a motorcycle. The accident had been blamed on a drunk sheriff's deputy. I was not convinced. I blamed her death on the stranger, on the aliens.

I had spent hours searching that valley near Ghost Mountain for some shred of evidence that would tie the aliens to Jaime's death. Then one evening, just before dark, I'd found it.

I'd spent almost an hour digging through tangled underbrush at the bottom of that hill where Jaime, one of the sheriff's deputies, and the mysterious man on the motorcycle had died. My arms and legs stung with tiny scratches, perforated trails of blood along bare skin. The overhead sky was rusty red. I was about to start for home when I saw something gleaming on the ground.

Filled with excitement and this strange, surreal sense that I had just turned the corner into the *Twilight Zone*, I walked around to the back of the kitchen, opened the door to the basement, and started down into darkness. The sight of the weathered brick walls and the musty smell of the earth greeted me. I started down. I started down the stairs into the basement.

A blast of thunder--cannon fire from a pirate ship--tumbled through the void overhead.

In an earlier time, the basement had been a secret hideout for pirates, a bunker in which to wait out a nuclear war, a mad scientist's lab, and a mummy's tomb. That last metaphor seemed to suit it best. I thought of Howard Carter and his group opening King Tut's tomb.

"What do you see?" someone had asked Carter who was shining a light through an opening in the wall.

"Wonderful things!" the archaeologist had exclaimed as he looked upon the gleaming wonders within.

I reached the foot of the steps. I pulled a string and a bare light bulb came to life. Stacked in the corner of the basement was a trove--the amassed treasures of a very happy and all-too-brief childhood. I moved a box of sports equipment, an ice cream freezer, and a bag of Halloween decorations out of the way. I picked up a folded badminton net and set it up against the wall. The top of my old toy box was cleared. I opened it.

Inside lay the tangled bodies of G.I. Joes, DC and Marvel superheroes, the Six Million Dollar Man, the *Star Trek* crew, Big Jim and his Pack, Johnny West and Geronimo, and Evel Knievel with his cycles and launchers. For a moment I stood transfixed. Then I knelt down and, slowly and reverently, began to move the dormant shapes of my old friends aside. There, beneath the layer of toys, lay the shoebox. My hands were trembling a bit as I picked it up. I pulled it out into the light. The box was taped shut, but the tape had grown dry with time. I peeled it away without much trouble and removed the lid. Inside lay a die-cast Eagle lander from the *Space 1999* series, a diploma from StarFleet Academy that I had ordered in the mail when I was a young space cadet, my first *Superboy and the Legion of Superheroes* comic book, and three other items: a cassette tape, an amber-colored piece of a broken turn signal light, and something wrapped in aluminum foil. Slowly, with shaking hands, I removed the foil.

I couldn't believe it. It could not possibly be true, yet it was. It was a CD ROM--technology from the 1990s. How could it have possibly made it back to 1977?

I rewrapped the CD and placed it back into the box. I set the shoebox on the bottom stair. I closed the toy box and placed everything back on top. Then I shut off the lights, picked up the shoebox, and walked back up the stairs. My mother was still washing dishes.

"Could I use your computer?" I asked.

"It's right there," Mom said. Dad had set up a small workstation in the corner of the kitchen.

I seated myself in the chair and switched on the computer. I dropped the CD into the tray and heard the drive come on. I accessed the CD ROM drive. The drive began to whir. Then the computer let out an annoying squawk.

PLEASE ENTER THE PASSWORD NOW.

"Oh, great!" I said. I stifled the desire to use more colorful words.

"What is it?" Mom asked.

"This is crazy," I told her. "I found this CD ROM back in 1977 close to where Jaime died. As far as I know, they didn't even have CDs back then."

"A mystery," Mom said. "What's on it?"

"I don't know," I said. "It's password protected."

I heard another blast of thunder. Wind blew rain against the kitchen windows. I *had* to know what was on that CD, and I needed the help of an expert. Fortunately I had a pretty good idea where I could find one.

Chapter 2: Of Time Warps and Close Encounters

The phone rang twice.

"Hello," a familiar voice said.

"Larry," I said. "This is James. I'm sorry to call you at this hour."

'That's okay," he said. "I was out here in the shop working on something. Where are you?"

"At home," I said. "My folks' house, actually."

"You're in Arkansas?" he said.

"Yeah," I said. "Listen, Larry. I've got something I need to show you. I really need your help."

"Come on over," he said. I could hear the smile in his voice. "I'll put on some coffee."

Larry Christopher, my childhood friend, had never left Miracle Springs. He dropped out of college when his wife Susan had become pregnant with their son. Now he's a helicopter pilot and mechanic, flying and maintaining the chopper used by Miracle Springs Medical Center. He also runs a small TV/VCR repair shop in his converted garage. He also invents things. He's gotten several patents, but none of them has translated into the financial success he's hoped for.

It was about one o'clock when I pulled into the drive in front of Larry's repair shop. There was a light on inside. I knocked.

"Come in," I heard him say. I opened the door and smelled the coffee brewing—coffee mixed with the burnt, acrid smell of solder. At first I didn't see Larry. Two big worktables ran through the center of the refurbished garage. They were piled with television sets, VCRs, and—I noticed—a few computers and synthesizers as well. The walls were lined with shelves. Larry was on the far end of the room working in the soft glare of a fluorescent lamp. He was holding a soldering gun and working to the rhythm of Christopher Cross singing "Ride Like the Wind." When he saw me, he set down the gun and walked toward me. His narrow face broke into a big smile.

"Good to see ya, man," he said. He extended a hand, and we shook. Larry showed me some things he had been working on in his spare time. He had been learning to repair computers lately and had kept up his childhood hobby of building flying model rockets and radio-controlled airplanes. He showed me the latest pictures of his family and told me what was going on in Miracle Springs. Finally he motioned me toward a beat-up captain's chair and poured us both some coffee.

"Now," he said. "What was it your were going to show me?"

I pulled out the CD ROM and held it into the light.

"I found this on Ghost Mountain about a month after Jaime died," I told him. Then I let it sink in. He took the CD, looked at it, and shook his head.

"They didn't have these in 1977, Jim."

"These files are password protected," I said. "I have to know what's in them. Do you think you can break the encryption?"

"Maybe," he said. "But it'll take time."

I fell asleep on Larry's battered couch while he worked into the night. I dreamed Jaime and I were standing in a clearing with a lot of other people. Cars from the seventies were parked all around us and people were staring up into the sky. It was night, but the sky was full of lights. Something hovered directly overhead, something huge. It had a soft roar that seemed to drown out everything. A soft wind blew Jaime's hair around.

Vibrations seemed to go all the way through our bodies. Then the lights on the belly of the UFO started flashing. Sounds started coming from it . . . five musical tones. *Dah da duh da dahhhh!*

"That's it!" something inside me said. I sat up on the couch. "That's it! *Close Encounters!* The mountain and the UFOs and everything."

"What?" Larry asked. He looked at me like I'd lost my mind.

"Okay," I took a deep breath. "In *Close Encounters* the UFOs were fixated on Devil's Tower, Wyoming. In Miracle Springs, the UFOs are always seen over Ghost Mountain. If the person who saved those files was a science fiction fan . . . "

"But how do you know this CD has anything to do with Ghost Mountain or aliens?" he asked.

"A hunch," I said. "That's all. Just a hunch."

"More like a blind leap," Larry said.

I sat down in front of the computer.

"Okay. I'll try passwords associated with *Close Encounters.*" For several minutes I tried words like "Encounters," "Devil's Tower," and "Spielberg." I even tried out the names of characters and actors. Nothing worked.

"Give it up, Jim," Larry said. "This isn't getting anywhere."

"*Gafac!*" I yelled.

"What is *gafac*?" he asked. "Klingon profanity?"

"No, *b'takh*," I told him. "It's the five musical tones from the movie. G-A-F-A-C."

He rolled his eyes.

"Whatever you say."

I typed in the five letters, and hit the return key.

The computer whirred, and the file opened.

"Well, I'll be a—"

Inside was a collection of other files. I clicked on one of the folder icons. A word-processing document opened.

"An Exploration of the Atmospheric Phenomena Surrounding Ghost Mountain," the title read. "by John Tarkington, PhD."

"Tarkington?" I said.

"From the university?" Larry asked. "He's a character."

"I just met him," I said. I shook my head. "I must have mixed up the disks, . . . but I don't remember him giving me a disk."

"That must be what happened though," Larry said. "There's no way this came from 1977. It's just not possible."

"There are some other files here," I said.

He clicked on them. A series of digital photographs opened. One of them showed a pretty girl in a blue bikini standing beside a picnic table. Another showed a young man in an orange life vest being pulled behind a ski boat. One showed Dr. Tarkington wearing a Hawaiian shirt and sunglasses. He was laughing and flipping hamburgers on a grill.

"These look like scenes from a picnic," Larry said. I opened homework assignments and some music files.

"This belonged to Keith Anderson," I finally said.

"The student who was killed a few weeks ago?" Larry said.

"Yeah," I said. "There's something else here." I clicked on the last folder. I clicked on a few files and realized they were documents and images downloaded from the internet.

"This is all about Ghost Mountain," I said. "Some kind of government cover-up."

"Don't believe everything you read," Larry said.

"What?" I said. "You used to think the government was behind everything."

"People change," he said.

"Hah," I said. I opened another file.

Project Timewarp: For Government Eyes Only

I read the abstract at the beginning.

"According to this file," I said, "there's a group of scientists experimenting with time travel."

"Oh, yeah," Larry said. "Like that could really happen. This is garbage, Jim. Throw that CD away or use it as a coaster, but don't take it seriously."

"Most of the time I'd agree with you," I said. "But there's something going on here. I really don't think I mixed up the CD ROMs. This one was still wrapped in foil when I brought it in—the same foil I wrapped it in back in 1977. This CD has been in the bottom of my toy box for nearly twenty years."

"That just can't be," Larry said. "I'm sorry."

"The police were in a high speed chase with a guy on a motorcycle," I said. "Jaime was right in the curve when Neeson lost control of his car and hit her and the guy on the bike. They all went into the canyon. The only one to survive was the guy driving the car."

"Jim. Come on."

"And nobody ever identified the guy on the bike," I said. "If he was the one carrying this CD . . ."

"Keith Anderson?" Larry said. "Back in 1977?"

"I know," I said. "It's crazy."

"Yeah," Larry said. "It's nuts."

"But there's one person who knows for sure."

* * *

"Dr. Tarkington, this is James Koslow."

It was nine o'clock the next morning when I called Tarkington from my parents' house.

"James," Tarkington said. "You can call me John—or Tark. Listen. The committee still hasn't made its decision yet. If it was up to me, we'd have hired you on the spot, but the rest of those guys have to talk everything to death. Just like a bunch of professors."

"That's not why I called."

"Oh. Really? What's up?"

"Okay," I said. "I had a friend who died back in 1977. A UFO was supposed to have appeared over Ghost Mountain and crashed outside of town. Well, some people said it was a UFO. Some said it was a helicopter that came out of a UFO. Anyway the police and a bunch of the locals went to investigate. One of the people from the UFO tried to escape on a motorcycle. A sheriff's deputy was chasing him in a police car when he accidentally struck him and killed him—along with a twelve-year-old girl. That girl was a good friend of mine."

"That's—that's terrible," Tarkington said.

"When I was a kid, I blamed the accident on aliens," I told him. "I spent days going over the place where it had happened. The police had already cleaned the place up, but they didn't find everything. Several feet away, in a tangle of brush, I found something. I didn't know what it was, because it wasn't supposed to have been invented yet, but it was a CD ROM. I think it belonged to your student, to Keith Anderson."

Tarkington didn't say anything.

"He didn't really fall out of a helicopter, did he?"

"I—we can't talk about this," Tarkington said. "I'm sorry. I wish I could. I—I'll call you about the job when we know something, but we can't talk about this."

He hung up.

I called Larry.

"Yeah."

"I just talked to Tarkington."

"And?"

"He said he couldn't talk about it."

"He couldn't talk about it?"

"Yeah. He sounded nervous, like somebody else might be listening in."

"I don't know what we've stumbled into," Larry said. "But I doubt it has anything to do with time travel."

"I don't think he's going to talk to us," I said. "But he's not the only person who knows what happened that night."

* * *

"It's a silver disk about . . . . . just under five inches in diameter. There's writing on one side. CD-RW. The other side is silver, and there's a hole in the middle. It looks kind of like a record, but it's smooth. There aren't any grooves. I don't know what it is, but I'm going to find out. If

it takes the rest of my life, I swear I'll find out what really happened to Jaime."

I ejected the cassette from the tape deck.

"Do you still think I dreamed all of this up?" I asked.

Larry didn't say anything.

I pulled into the parking lot of a convenience store and bait shop that lay on the shore of Gleason Lake.

Billy Neeson had been running the store for over ten years. He had broken both legs in the accident that had taken the lives of Jaime, the unknown man on a motorcycle, and Deputy Beavers. He had survived the accident, the doctor had said, because he was drunk and flexible. He had also caused the accident and had spent three years in prison for this.

It was Saturday morning. Several trucks with empty boat trailers were already parked in the lot beside the boat ramp. Billy's Stop-n-Go was a cinderblock building with gas pumps out front and a screen door. A bell rang as Larry and I stepped inside.

"What kin I do fer ya?" a skinny, middle-aged man behind the counter asked us. His face looked leathered and old but his hair was still light brown.

"Are you Billy Neeson?" I asked.

"Yessir," he said. "I reckon I am. What kin I do fer you fellas?"

"I'm James Koslow," I said. "This is Larry Christopher. We've got something we need to talk to you about."

"Y'all ain't policemen, are ya?" he asked. "If ya are, I got nothin' to hide. I don't even sell beer here no more. Not since I stopped drinkin'."

"We're not policemen," I said. "We wanted to ask you some questions about the night of the helicopter crash on Ghost Mountain." His eyes widened, then narrowed. The gears in his mind began to turn.

"Y'all ain't reporters, are ya?" he asked. "Listen. I done told the reporters ever'thang I knew."

"We're not reporters," I said. "Actually we were friends of the little girl who died."

Neeson looked down at the counter. His shoulders sagged.

"Y'all just don't know," he said. He shook his head. "Y'all just don't know. I've dreamed about that purdy little girl on and off for fifteen years. I can't never git her face out of my mind. I nearly drunk myself to death over it once, but then the Lord got aholt of me. I know He's forgiven me, but I don't know if I can ever forgive myself—not completely, anyways."

"Can you tell us what happened?" I asked.

"When we got there," he said, "that hellycopter was all piled up in some bushes. It had been tore up pretty bad when it crashed. One of the men banged up his head pretty seriously, but the other three was okay. They was just shook up."

"What did they look like?" Larry asked.

"Like regular folks," Neeson shrugged. "They dressed a little funny though—'cept one guy in a Hawaiian shirt. He was dressed like Magnum P.I. The rest of 'em looked like they was from Russia or somewhere over there maybe. Haircuts kind of different and all. The police and fire department showed up around the same time we did. The sheriff was there too. I think he suspected 'em of haulin' dope, so he asked for some ID. That was the weirdest part of all."

"Why?"

"Their IDs was phony. They was from 1997 or sometime around then. But if you're gonna go to the trouble to make fake ID, why would you put the wrong dates on 'em? It don't make no kind of sense."

"You're right," Larry shrugged. "It don't." I elbowed him.

"Anyways, the sheriff wanted to take 'em into custody. One of the men panicked. He got on a motorcycle somebody had parked in the clearing there, and took off on it. I got in my car, and took off after 'im. I 'spose I was too drunk to use good judgment. I was so revved up about the whole thing, that I follered the fella too fast. If he'da tried to pull over, I'da run over 'im, so there wasn't nothin' he could do but go faster. That was when we came into that curve. He hit the little girl, I hit both of 'em, and we all went over the clift. I don't even remember any of that."

"Look," I said. "I'm sorry to bring up bad memories."

"S'all right," he said. "Guess it's what I git for bein' so stupid back then."

"What happened to those men?" Larry asked. "The ones who crashed."

"Sheriff took 'em downtown," Neeson said. "Then, near as I understand it, the Air Force come and got 'em. Nobody ever saw 'em anymore after that. Then it wasn't two months until the guvment bought up the land around Ghost Mountain and had it all fenced off. Tell me there wasn't no connection to that now!"

"Makes sense to me," I said.

The bell rang as another customer came in. Perfect timing.

"Thanks for talking to us," I said.

"Yer welcome," Neeson said. "You boys come back anytime."

Larry and I walked back out to Larry's waiting jeep.

"He's actually not a bad sort," I said. "All these years I kind of despised him for being a drunk and all."

"Yeah," Larry said. "Me too."

Our next stop was the foot of Ghost Mountain. We drove up the road until we were only a few feet from the guard shack there. We pulled over beside the road, got out, and walked up to the gate. A young man in military clothing stepped out with a rifle on his shoulder. Another man watched through a window which, I'd guess, was made of bulletproof glass.

"Sir," the young man with the rifle told us, "I'm going to have to ask you to get back into your vehicle and leave. This is a restricted area."

"We need to talk to whoever is in charge of this installation," I told him. "Where would we go to do that?"

"That information is classified," he said. "But you might want to talk to Lieutenant Starkey at Braxton Air Force Base. He's in charge of security here."

"Thanks," I said.

We drove an hour to get to Braxton. Lieutenant Starkey, it turned out, had the weekend off.

"That's okay," I told the man on duty. "Just tell him to get this to his superior." I passed him an envelope. "Get it to whoever knows what's really going on at Ghost Mountain. We think he might be interested." Inside the envelope was a copy of the CD ROM and information about where and *when* I had found it.

* * *

Larry and I drove around town talking and speculating. I made it home a little after seven o'clock. My mother met me at the door.

"Dr. Tarkington just called," she said. "He wants you to meet him at the university."

"Did he say what it was about?" I asked.

"No," she said. "I thought it must be about the job, but I didn't ask. I didn't think I should."

"That's okay," I said. "I'll give him a call and see where he wants me to meet him."

"How's Larry?" Mom asked.

"He's fine," I said. "Busy as usual."

"Did he tell you anything about the accident?"

"The helicopter accident?" I said. "Not much. Why?"

"Larry was on that expedition," she said. "He was the pilot."

* * *

The sun was starting to set when I made it back to Green Mountain University. I stepped inside the science building. The walls were covered in gray marble and the air had a chemical scent. Tarkington met me just inside. With him were two other men. They were dressed in civilian clothes, but I knew they weren't just students. Something in their manner told me they were either policemen or military.

"So what's this about?" I asked.

"Not here," he said. I followed him through the empty building. We passed cases of fossilized dinosaur bones, samples of petrified rocks, planetary displays. We took a ride up the elevator to the third floor. He led me down the hall and into a meeting room with a large table. The two men who had been escorting us waited outside as we went in.

A tall broad-shouldered man in a uniform stepped up to meet us as we entered. He had a broad, blunt face that was homely in a kind, honest sort of way. He smiled, kind of a sad serious smile, and extended his hand.

"Come on in, Dr. Koslow," he said. "I'm Colonel Holden. It's good to meet you."

"Thanks," I said.

"And I believe you already know Larry Christopher."

"You were the pilot on that expedition," I said. "Why didn't you tell me?"

"Because it's classified," Colonel Holden said. "Before we go any further, I need to know exactly how much you know and how you found out."

I hesitated. I wondered if he would have me killed if I knew too much. Somehow, though, I felt I could trust him.

"I think you're guarding some kind of time machine there on Ghost Mountain," I told him. "I think someone went through it into the past and caused the accident that killed my friend."

He didn't say anything.

"That's an incredible story," he said. "Where did you get it?"

"I found a CD ROM near the scene of Jaime's accident," I told him. "That was back in 1977. We didn't have CD ROMS back then."

"Are you sure that CD came from 1977?" he asked. "Your memory may be playing tricks on you."

"That CD ROM has been in the bottom of my toy chest for over 20 years," I told him. "I'm absolutely certain about that. Now I want to know where it came from."

"Why is it so important?" Holden asked me.

"Jaime Mitchell died in a traffic accident twenty years ago," I said. "I believe that accident was caused by visitors from the future, people who didn't belong in that time. That accident wasn't supposed to have happened and, if you know how, I want you to use your machine to send me back in time and let me stop it from happening."

"Are you willing to go through our screening process?" he asked. "Psychiatric exams? Medical exams?"

I was amazed that he had asked me. Was he admitting that my wild theory was true?

"Yes," I told him. "I'm willing"

He nodded.

"How many people have traveled through time?" I asked.

"Ten manned expeditions," he said. "Most of them only went through for a few moments, looked around, and returned. We've done most of our studies with unmanned probes. It's safer that way."

"So what's the secret?" I asked. "How did you build a time machine?"

"We didn't," Tarkington said, suddenly cutting in. "It's been there for centuries waiting for us to discover it."

"Where?" I asked. Then it came to me. "Ghost Mountain?"

"Exactly," he said. "Those lights aren't alien spacecraft or fairies. They're disturbances in space-time."

"But how did they get there?" I asked. "Some kind of device left behind by aliens?"

"Like *Chariots of the Gods* or *Stargate*?" he asked. "We wondered that ourselves but, as near as we can determine, the time portals on Ghost Mountain weren't something anybody invented."

"They're some kind of natural phenomenon that our physicists are still trying to make sense of," Holden explained. "They've shaken every model we've had about time and the universe. They were discovered by accident when a university research team accidentally passed through one of those holes in time in a helicopter and ended up back in 1977."

"That's what happened to you?" I turned to Tarkington. "That's how Anderson died?"

"Yeah," he said. "It happened about six weeks ago. We'd gotten permission to study the phenomena over Ghost Mountain. We'd rented a helicopter. Larry, here, was our pilot. It was just about sunset when one of those lights appeared hovering over the mountain. It was this huge, pulsating sphere. Biggest one I'd seen yet. We started to move in. That's when we picked something up on the radio. It was KJAM, one of the local stations."

"Beau Leggs was broadcasting from Miracle Mountain Amusement Park," Larry said.

"Beau Leggs?" I said.

"Do you remember him?" Larry asked.

"Yeah," I said. "Big sunglasses and an afro. Hawaiian shirts." We all looked at Tarkington.

"So he's got good taste in fashion," Tarkington shrugged.

"That was back in the seventies," I said. "Back in the days of 'I'm Your Boogie Man' and 'Shake Your Booty.' And Miracle Mountain Park shut down in the early eighties."

"I thought at first that the station was replaying an old broadcast," he said. "Then I realized it was coming from the anomaly. Collins, one of the other men, started talking about how our TV and radio messages travel out into space. He wondered if aliens had picked them up and were trying to use them to communicate with us."

"But that doesn't make sense," I said. "If the lights on Ghost Mountain were aliens, they would have been here for centuries. You'd think they'd have learned the language by now."

"That's what I said," Larry said.

"We were carrying some experimental scanning equipment," Tarkington said. "High tech stuff like your NASA guys would use. When we fired it up, it was like dropping a match in a powder keg. There was a power spike. The copter's electrical system went haywire. The next thing I knew, we were falling out of the sky. Larry was struggling for altitude, but everything had shorted out. We crashed on one of the other mountains, landed in a grove of trees. When the police showed up, I noticed everything looked out of date. The clothes, hairstyles, and cars were all about twenty years out of style. They started asking us questions. I didn't know if I should answer them. Finally they asked for some identification. When they saw the dates on it, they just went crazy. Started calling us Russians and threatening to arrest us."

"Like people from Russia don't know what year it is?"

"That's when Keith panicked," Tarkington said. "He got away from us, stole a motorcycle, and led the police on that chase down the mountain. The guy driving the police car was drunk. He ended up killing Keith, your friend Jaime, and the guy in the car with him."

"What happened to the rest of you?" I asked.

"We were taken into custody by the Air Force. We managed to convince them of our story. Working together with them, we found a way to harness the portals."

"But how?" I asked. "You don't even know how they work."

"We do know how they work," Tarkington said. "We just don't know why. They open at random. Most of the time they're only open for a fraction of a second. Sometimes they stay open for several minutes. Most are too small to travel through. It's the big ones that can actually serve as functioning portals."

"What about the tidal forces?" I asked. "In, like, a black hole you'd be pulled apart by the gravity."

"Apparently not a problem with these," he said.

"But why hasn't anyone ever been trapped in the past before?" I asked. "The ghost-images people have reported seeing on the mountain never stayed around for long."

"That's what we wondered at first," Tarkington said. "Then we realized something in our scanning equipment had somehow magnified the effect."

"But how could you use them?" I asked. "You had no way of knowing when one of those holes in time would open."

"We used radio waves," he said. "Back in 1977 we mounted a radio transmitter on the mountain. It constantly transmits the time and date. We also mounted antennas all over the mountain. If a time portal opens up near one of these antennas, it picks up the radio waves that come through. If the portal leads to anywhere after we set up the transmitter in 1977, we can determine the exact time and date the portal leads to. Sometimes we can visit earlier times too if we pick up radio and TV signals and are able to tell by the contents when they were transmitted. If we pick up part of an episode of *The Lucy Show* and can find the air date, we can determine the time."

"Unless it's a rerun," I said.

"If you're lucky," he said, "you get part of an advertisement too. That helps narrow it down more. Anyway the idea of using radio and television signals to determine where the portals lead came from what happened to us that night. We heard that Beau Leggs broadcast from 1977 coming out of the portal even before we went through it. The range was limited, but a receiver located right near the mouth of one of the portals could still pick it up.

It occurred to us that we could deliberately send messages to ourselves through the portals and use the information to plan our trips."

"More recently," Larry said, "they've started firing microchip timers into the anomalies."

"Microchip timers?"

"Yeah," he said. "A microchip with a timer on it. It records the date on which it was sent. Then, when it arrives in the past, it starts counting down. They can recover it later and find the date and time on which it was sent and where it ended up."

"But what if somebody in the past found it?" I asked.

"They wouldn't know what it was," Tarkington said. "We're talking about something the size of a mosquito. Unless you knew how to scan for the tracers on them, you'd never find them."

"But how could you plan the trips?" I asked. "If you know a portal opened up between yesterday and the day before, it wouldn't be of any use to you, because both of those dates would be in the past."

"We thought of that too," Tarkington said. "In addition to the time and date, the transmitter on the mountain also transmits an encrypted log of all of the time anomalies we know about. It's a high-speed record of when the anomalies appear, how big they are, how long the portals stay open, and where they lead. That way, if a time portal opens to the future, we can get a log of time portals that have not yet opened. I will, in effect, get a message from next week telling me that a time portal to yesterday will open later today."

"But what about the return trip?" I asked.

"Simple," Larry said. "If you knew that a time portal to June 1988 was going to be opening tomorrow and that a portal to July 1988 was going to be opening next week, you can plan a round trip. You'd be there a month and be gone a week."

"Why did you decide to tell me all of this?" I finally asked. "I couldn't have proven that CD ROM was from the past. You could have just denied the whole thing."

"You're a physicist," Tarkington said. "You've worked for NASA. We'd like to have you on the team studying these things with us. You showed up here at just the right time."

"You called me," I told him. "Remember? You said you'd heard about me from people in Miracle Springs."

"Yes," he said. "That's true."

"One of those people wouldn't happen to be a helicopter mechanic, would he?" I asked. Larry smiled.

"Could be," Tarkington said.

"Who better to recommend you?" Larry said.

"You could have told me earlier today," I said.

"We were still discussing it," Holden said. "You figured things out a little bit quicker than we expected."

"Back to my original request," I said. "Is there any way you can send me back to save Jaime?"

"We would like to," Colonel Holden said. "If we can."

"When the Air Force gave me permission to explore those lights," Tarkington said, "they knew what they were. What's more, they knew what was going to happen to my team when we crashed back in 1977. They didn't tell me."

"We tried to protect them without telling them too much," Holden said.

"Any interference with the expedition could have changed history and kept us from discovering those time portals," Tarkington said. He sounded bitter about it. "The discovery was too important to let that happen, so they sent Keith Anderson to his death."

"In the original scenario," Holden explained, "there was a gun in the chopper. When the police surrounded them, Keith Anderson pulled the gun and used it to hold the police at bay while he escaped into the crowd. When Tarkington and his group applied for permission to study the phenomena, we didn't allow them to carry any weapons on board the chopper. We didn't explain why, but we thought we could stop the accident by preventing Anderson from having easy access to a gun."

"It didn't work," I said.

"No," Holden said. "He didn't have a gun on the chopper so he took one from one of the policemen instead. It almost makes you wonder if he was destined to die, if the accident was destined to happen."

"No," Tarkington said. "I can't accept that."

"Wait," I said. "Time out. You're saying this is some kind of repeating cycle?"

"Right," Tarkington said. "In the first 1977, there was no UFO crash. They would have seen the light, but no helicopter. Then 1997 came around, we encountered the time warp and got tossed into the past. There was a gun in the chopper. Anderson pulled it out, and got himself killed. 1997 rolled around again. This time the mountain was controlled by the Air Force. We had to get permission to fly over it, but weren't allowed to have a gun. Anderson took one from a cop, and got himself killed anyway."

"Do we know for sure that this is only the third cycle?" Holden asked. "We might have repeated the same sequence hundreds of times without knowing it."

"And you're thinking there's no way out?" I asked. "That all of this is destiny and Anderson and Jaime will die regardless?"

"I hope I'm wrong," Holden said. "If I am, there may still be a way to save Anderson and Jaime both that won't interfere with the discovery of the portals."

"What is it?" I asked.

"In three weeks," he said, "there is a time portal opening up between our time and May 27, 1977. We could send someone through. That person could go through, get there a week before the helicopter crash, and find a way to save both Keith and Jaime. Another portal opens the day after the crash. The traveler could use this one to return to 1997."

"We're planning to send somebody back," Tarkington said. "I thought of going myself. Then you showed up. You know the 1977 version of Miracle Springs better than I do. I didn't grow up here."

"We've seen how dangerous time travel can be," Holden said. "We can't ask you to take the risk. You don't know what you could end up doing to your own past—and present."

"What about it?" Tarkington asked me. "Do you want to go back?"

"Yes," I told him. I prayed that I wasn't making a terrible mistake.

Chapter 3: Arrival

"What was it like?" I asked Larry later. "Traveling through time?"

"Like passing through a cloud," he told me. "Passing through a cloud."

The next three weeks were exhausting. Every private thought, every secret motive, every dream, idea, and belief I had was dragged into the examiner's light. I felt as if my soul had been laid bare. Finally it was over. To my total disbelief, I had passed. I had been approved for a trip into the past. The only thing left to do was pray to a merciful God I wouldn't foul things up too badly.

* * *

Deputy Billy Neeson, the best I can reconstruct things, was parked in the gravel driveway of Welcome Baptist Church. The church, located on a winding mountain road, was deserted. The late spring air was hot. Billy had the window down and the radio playing. He was drunk. A half-empty bottle of Jack Daniels was wedged between his skinny thighs.

With so little work to do in the small Arkansas town of Miracle Springs, Billy had spent many evenings this way.

The sun was a burning red ball throwing glistening shafts of light through the dark tops of the pine trees that stood around the edges of the cemetery. Whippoorwills called and crickets chirped amid the stones. The universe seemed so still that Billy almost thought he could feel the world turning under him. Of course, that could have been a side effect of his drinking.

Then Billy heard something—a loud thumping like helicopter blades.

He jerked up in his seat, craned his neck over the steering wheel so he could peer through the very top of the windshield.

A ball of light hovered, ghostlike, above Ghost Mountain. A helicopter emerged from the glare and vanished below the tree line.

Billy grabbed the radio.

"Breaker, breaker, one-nine," he said. "Deputy Billy Neeson reporting. I have just saw an unidentified flying object and am going in hot pursuit. Durn aliens are usin' helicopters now. Come back."

He didn't wait for a reply. Billy woke the car, a hulking LTD, with a frantic twist of the key. He slammed it into gear, spun it out into the road with gravel and dirt flying sideways, went down a hill, missed a turn, and piled the car up in a ditch. Steam rose over the edge of the embankment.

* * *

"Take a look, Jim," Larry said. We're home."

The sun was almost down. Larry edged the helicopter away from Ghost Mountain. I could see Miracle Springs below us.

"Is this really the past?" I asked.

"Look," Larry said. "There's the drive-in and the Tastee Freeze."

"And Miracle Mountain Park," I said. "We're really here." It seemed impossible.

Larry maneuvered the helicopter over to a large clearing on one of the neighboring mountains. He would have about two minutes to unload me and make it back to the portal before it closed. At Larry's expert bidding, the craft dropped smoothly into a clearing. It touched down on a plateau of bare dirt with a cliff wall on one side and embankments leading down into the forest on the other three. Some oil tanks, a sludge pit, and a grasshopper pump shared the plateau with the thundering helicopter. Dust and small rocks whirled around us.

"Let's get your stuff together," Larry yelled over the engine noise.

I followed him through a hatch in the back of the passenger cabin. My motorcycle was strapped into a compartment over one of the skids. Larry handed me my backpack and helped me unstrap the bike. I put on my pack, rolled the bike down the ramp to the salty-smelling earth, moved away from the helicopter, and looked back.

Larry and the others waved at me from inside. I could tell Larry really wanted to stay too, but hiding the helicopter in the past would have been difficult. The vehicle lifted off and thumped its way back to Ghost Mountain.

The helicopter's engine noise vanished. In the silence that followed, a stab of fear went through me. I was a stranger here, a stranger from another time. I had no way of getting myself back.

Pushing those thoughts away, I took a deep breath and looked around at the pine trees and hardwoods, at the creek that ran below the road I was on. I was home. This was a fine Arkansas evening in late spring, and I was home.

I kick-started my bike, twisted the throttle, and made my way to a dirt road that led around the cliff that overlooked the oil well site. I followed the road that led to and from the oil tanks, found the main road, and turned onto it. I had gone less than a mile when I found Billy Neeson's squad car in a ditch. Steam was still rising from the engine.

When Billy told me he'd seen a U.F.O. spitting out helicopters, my heart nearly stopped beating. The horror stories of time travel gone bad rose up in my mind. Billy could have killed himself trying to reach the spot where we had landed. He might still lose his job for wrecking the car anyway. I smiled inwardly. If he lost his job, he'd never be involved in the chase. Just seeing the helicopter might have been enough to put things right. I sighed. That would be too easy.

I rode past Welcome Baptist Church, down the mountainside, and into Miracle Springs. The Ben Franklin store and the Tastee Freeze drive-in were still doing business. *Rocky* was playing at the drive-in. *Star Wars* was showing at the Cameo Theater and *Close Encounters of the Third Kind* was "coming soon."

Miracle Lake and the amusement park were on the other side of town. I'd see them soon enough.

I passed the Methodist Church where my parents had dragged my brothers and me to Sunday School all of those mornings.

I pulled into Harkins E-Z Stop just to have a look around. Mr. Benson and Mr. Kilpatrick were sitting there talking about a horse Mr. Benson had just bought. The two old men eyed me a little suspiciously as I walked in.

"How's it going?" I asked them.

"Fine," Mr. Kilpatrick said.

"Just fine," Mr. Benson said.

I smiled so much they probably thought I was laughing at them, but nothing could have been farther from the truth. I was really here. These men had been dead for years but here, in this time, they were still alive.

I went to the cooler and noticed that most of the drinks were in glass bottles. There was only one kind of Coke and that was plain old basic Coca-cola. Diet Coke, Caffeine Free Coke, Caffeine Free Diet Coke, and Cherry Coke were still years away.

The canned drinks all had tabs with metal rings on them, but I preferred the glass bottles.

I pulled out a frosty 16-oz. Coke, got an Almond Hershey from the candy rack, and went to the check-out stand. A young woman stepped up to the cash register. I got a strange feeling of *deja' vu* when I saw her.

"Is that everything?" she asked.

"Yeah," I said. "That's it."

She rang up the total. I gave her some cash--nothing marked any later than 1976.

I watched her as she counted up the change. She was young, dark-haired, and naturally attractive even without make up. Her name was Lisa Mitchell. She was Jaime's mother. I hadn't remembered how pretty she was. Through a twelve-year-old boy's eyes, she had just been another adult woman.

"Here you go," she said. "Four dollars and fifteen cents." She slid the money into my hand.

"Thanks," I said.

"Come back," she said, smiling.

"Have you got a bottle opener?" I asked.

She passed me one. I popped the top off my Coke.

"Thanks."

I walked outside and sat down on my motorcycle. It was later than I had realized. The sun was down. Only the grayest hint of afterglow hung over the hills to the west. The streetlights were all glowing. I was unwrapping my Hershey bar when a familiar pale yellow Buick Riviera pulled into the parking lot and stopped at the gas pumps. The cars all seemed so big.

My heart hammered with anticipation as the car's doors began to open. A man in his late thirties climbed out, unscrewed the car's gas cap, unhooked the nozzle from the gas pump, turned on the pump, and started pumping gas. He was wearing knit pants and a wide belt. A woman in her thirties climbed out of the passenger side. Three boys wriggled around the rear seats and raced each other to the door of the store as their father went about filling his car with Gulf unleaded. The woman followed her sons into the store.

I tried not to stare, but I could hardly keep from it.

The boys were stair-stepped in age. The oldest was eleven. The middle one was ten. The youngest was seven.

I watched the oldest boy checking out the comic book rack with fanatical zeal. The other two were at the candy aisle.

"I can't believe we were ever that small," I whispered to myself. I watched my young alter-ego pull down an issue of the *Fantastic Four* and thumb through it. I'd forgotten about being that thin, having freckles and braces, and having so little taste in clothes. I still thought Toughskins with reinforced knees were as stylish as the next pair of pants.

My dad walked past my line of sight. He had dug out his wallet and was going through his bills.

My dad paid for the gas, for three pieces of candy, and for my comic book.

I watched the family--my family--climb into their car and drive away. They had never even noticed me. I finished my Coke and Hershey bar, kick-started my bike, and pulled out into the road. I started up a hill, the same one my family's pale yellow Riviera had just taken.

I went around a bend and pulled to a stop in front of a neat old frame house. I turned in, parked my bike at the base of the porch steps, killed the engine, and put down the kickstand.

I was so excited, I nearly ran to the porch. I knocked on the front door.

For a few seconds nothing happened. Then I heard footsteps. The porch light came on, and the front door swung open, then the screen door.

"Mr. Delaney!" I said. "It's great to see you again." I nearly grabbed him and hugged him. I'm not sure how he would have taken that, so I restrained myself and held out my hand instead. Leonard Delaney reached out slowly and shook my hand, but I could tell by the look on his face that he had no idea who I was.

"You look awful familiar," he said, ". . . but I've taught for so many years. Could you help an old man out?"

"James Koslow," I said. "From next door."

It took about two seconds for the name to register. Mr. Delaney's eyes opened wide.

"Wha-at?" he said. "I know a JIM Koslow next door, but he's only eleven years old."

And he knew my father's name wasn't James either.

"I know," I said. "I'm the Jim Koslow of 1997. I've come home as part of a time-travel expedition. I need your help."

A strange look formed on the teacher's face.

"Sure," he said. "What've you got in mind? Do we have to keep somebody from taking over the world or something like that?"

"Nothing that major," James Koslow of 1997 said. "I just need to stay with you for a while."

"Got any identification?" the teacher asked. "Driver's licence from the future or something?"

"It's all fake," I admitted. "I couldn't risk being stopped by the police. I can prove I'm from the future though."

"Just what I was hoping for," Mr. Delaney said. "Want to come in, or do you want me to get on your bike there and ride out to where you've got the time machine hidden?"

Or maybe, he thought, you've got a surprise retirement party set up somewhere for an old science teacher, and this little game is just the thing to get him there.

"I didn't use a time machine," I said. "There's a natural one outside of town."

His eyebrows went up.

"I got here in a helicopter," I told him. "It'll come back for me when this project's over. I can show you my evidence inside. It's nothing spectacular, but I think it will convince you."

"Good," Mr. Delaney said. "I was getting tired of standing out here. Come on in. Care for a glass of tea? A Coke maybe?"

"I just finished a Coke," I said. "Maybe later."

We walked through the living room and the hall and back into the den where *Charlie's Angels* was playing on the television set.

"Were you watching that?" I asked.

"I wasn't really into it," he admitted. "Just passing the time, I guess."

"Good," I said. "Because I've got something I want you to see."

I put my bag down on the floor and unzipped the top. I pulled out a few rolls of clothes and an overnight bag. Then I pulled out a portable camcorder and some tapes.

"This is a video camera," I told him. "They'll be invented in the early eighties. They're like a tape recorder with the picture. Can I hook it up to your T.V. set?"

"Sure," Mr. Delaney shrugged. He was rubbing his chin, watching with confused interest.

I disconnected the antenna and wired the camcorder into the back of his television set. I popped a tape into the machine.

"Sit down," I said. "You're going to enjoy this."

Reluctantly Mr. Delaney sat down in his easy chair. I went back to my bag, pulled out a remote control box, and sat down on the couch beside him. I touched the play button.

I'd put a few film clips on first. I had a few clips about Elvis sightings, some about the *Voyager* probe, some pictures of the Miracle Springs Christmas parade in 1996, and clips of several movies and television shows with high-tech special effects. I had clips from *Jurassic Park*, *Forrest Gump*, and one of the *Star Trek: The Next Generation* movies. Nothing I had shown him would radically alter history, but it would be expensive to fake.

I stopped the tape a few minutes into the *Star Trek* movie.

Static filled the screen.

"What do you think?" I asked.

He shook his head.

"You really are from the future," he said. His voice was quiet. "I never thought it could really happen, but it is true, isn't it? Somebody might be able to fake all of this. Maybe these VCR's have been invented, and they just aren't on the market yet. And maybe these movies are in the works and you're really a former student who works in Hollywood now and you're pulling a joke on me."

He shook his head, thought about it.

"But that's not what's going on, is it?" He sighed. "You really are Jim Koslow. You're older, but you're the same person. The way you say certain words . . . You've even got the walk down."

"What about my walk?" I asked.

"Well, nothing," he said. "It's distinctive. That's all."

"Oh."

"Why did you come back?" he asked.

"It's a long story," I said. "Can we turn off the TV?"
"Unless you want to watch *Charlie's Angels*," he said.
Jacklyn Smith appeared onscreen in a bikini.
"I'll record it," I told him.

Chapter 4: Catching Up on New Times

Mr. Delaney had poured some Folger's ground coffee into the filter of his Mr. Coffee, poured in the water, and flipped on the switch that set the coffee to brewing. The table was covered with a checkered vinyl tablecloth. I sat across from him and told him the rest--as much as I was allowed to tell anyway.

"I came back here to correct a mistake," I said. "I'm not the first. Well, I am the first to come here. The other expedition won't get here until next week, but in my time they already went back and caused an accident." I stopped. "This isn't making much sense is it?"

"I think I follow you," he said. "Somebody else came back and made some kind of mistake. You were sent back before them to stop it from happening."

"Exactly," I said. "That's it."

"So people in the 1990s just run back and forth through time?" he asked.

"Not exactly," I said. "Only a few people have. The general public doesn't even know. I found out by accident about three weeks ago, and I'm not really supposed to be here. Nobody's wanted to risk causing any of the major time paradoxes or other problems--the kind you see on movies like *Back to the Future*."

"I don't believe I've seen that one," he said.

I sighed.

"Of course you haven't," I said. "Silly me. I keep forgetting. It won't come out until 1985."

"Uh hunh."

He got up and walked over to the coffee maker.

"So are you here to stop a war or what?" he asked.

"No," I said. "No, it's a lot more personal than that. I came back to help a friend, a little girl named Jaime Mitchell."

"Mitchell," he said. "Does she go to school here?"

"No," I told him. "She just moved here. Right as the school year ended. She only visited on the last day of school. She's my age though. I mean she's the age of my 1977 counterpart. She's almost twelve."

"What happens to her?" he pulled the carafe from the coffee maker's burner, poured himself a cup of coffee. "Or what will happen to her?"

"She dies," I said. "In a traffic accident caused by some people from the university who traveled through time by mistake."

"Care for any coffee?" he asked.

I nodded.

"Yeah," I said. "Sugar and cream. I usually drink flavored coffee. Chocolate macadamia nut, that sort of thing."

"Chocolate coffee," he said. "Sounds interesting." He passed me the sugar, creamer, and a spoon.

"So they sent you back in time to stop the accident?" he asked.

"Yes," I said.

"Does any of this have anything to do with the UFO sightings lately?" he asked.

"Yes," I told him. "They're not visitors from space or anything like that. They're some kind of irregularities in the space-time continuum, holes in time that you can fly a helicopter through once you figure out when and where they're going to show up." I told him about the antenna and the transmitters.

"That's pretty ingenious," he said. I could tell he was still skeptical.

He brought me my coffee. The words "Number One Teacher" were printed on the mug.

"Thanks," I said, taking the mug from him. I looked at the words. "Did I give this to you for Christmas?"

"I wondered if you'd recognize it," he said. He was still testing me, testing the truth of my story.

He sat back down across from me. He had a coffee cup of his own.

"And you'll be here how long?" he asked.

"About five days," I said

"So what exactly happened that night--to the little girl, I mean?" he asked. "Or, maybe I should say, what happens to her?"

"She called me on the phone all excited," I said, ignoring the problem of verb tenses. "She said she'd seen a helicopter come out of a UFO, that it had crashed outside of town. She was going to get on her bike and try to get over there and wanted me to go with her. My folks were at the grocery store so I couldn't get them to take me. I told her I couldn't go."

"That was smart," Mr. Delaney said.

"Maybe," I said. "But she was really disappointed. She said she would wait for me, but she must have gotten impatient. She went on without me."

I shook my head. It was a little while before I could go on.

"She got on her bike and started down the road. She got to that hairpin curve just above the store and ran right into a high-speed chase. A guy on a motorcycle was trying to outrun the police. Billy Neeson was chasing him—high as a kite. Jaime was right in the curve when the car plowed into her and the biker. They all went over the cliff, and everybody but Neeson was killed."

Mr. Delaney was nodding. I reached into my backpack and pulled out a news clipping, an obituary. He took the clipping and read it. He took a sip of coffee and thought for a while.

"And you've been haunted by this whole thing for years?"

"If I'd agreed to meet her, she would still have been waiting for me at the store."

"You couldn't know that," he said.

"No," I said. "Of course I couldn't. But I still can't help thinking about. I learned to live with it. Or I thought I had. Then I realized none of it was supposed to have ever happened. The life I had lived was the result of a mistake. Jaime wasn't supposed to die and my childhood wasn't supposed to end that way."

"How did you know it was a mistake?" he asked.

"I found something at the place Jaime died," I told him. "I thought it was some kind of small, silver record. It was a kind of storage medium that won't be invented until the early 1990's or so. I'd had it for years but never realized what it was. Then suddenly I knew." I told him about my visit home, about finding the disk, about Larry and me breaking through the decryption, and about everything that had happened after that.

"And now you're here."

"Now I'm here."

"Hoo boy," Mr. Delaney shook his head. "Boy howdy. Never thought I'd hear anything like this." He got up, still holding his mug, and walked over to the window over the sink. It was open. The chirping of the crickets was loud that night. "So what's life like in the future? Obviously we haven't been invaded by the Russians yet."

"The Soviet Union collapsed in the early '90s," I told him. "It was hit hard by economic problems, and the countries forming it split apart."

"Wow," he said. "Who would have believed it?"

"And the Berlin wall's been torn down. Germany's been reunited."

"Sounds like a good time to be alive," he said. "No Cold War. A free Germany. How's your family in the future? Can I ask that?"

"They're all fine," I said. "My brothers are both married. Jason's got two children and working for an oil company. Barry's an emergency room nurse, and he's thinking about buying a cattle farm."

"What about yourself, Jim?" he asked. "You got a family?"

"No," I said. "I'm still in school." I thought about my apartment, of the nights spent alone there. "No. Just me."

"So what are you doing with yourself?"

"I got a doctorate in astrophysics," I told him. "I've been working for NASA in Houston."

His eyes lit up.

"NASA!" he said. "That's wonderful."

"It's not as glamorous as it sounds," I said.

"Nothing ever is," he said. "Still—NASA! One of my students. That's great."

"I'm thinking about teaching college now," I told him. "Following in your footsteps."

"That sounds good too," he said. "Play for the major leagues, then coach for a while."

He took a long swallow from his mug and asked the question I was afraid he would ask.

"I--uh--don't suppose I'll still be around by the time your era gets here," he said.

I tried to think of something to say, but couldn't. There was only one reason Colonel Holden and the others had allowed me to tell him everything about our mission. He would die of a heart attack in less than six months, and the secret of time travel would die with him.

"That's a long time," I found myself saying after I'd already waited too long, after I'd let the silence answer for me.

"I guess it was too much to hope for," he said, sighing. "Thanks for being honest with me anyway. It's kind of a relief, really. I don't think I'd want to live alone for another twenty years or so." He looked out the window. "It would have been nice to have heard about those *Voyager* probes, to have had one of those camcorder things, . . . to have seen you kids grow up."

"I feel like I've handed you your death sentence," I said. "I wish there was something I could tell you, some kind of assurance."

"It's okay," he said. "I've got my assurance. I'll be in a better place. I've always believed that."

"Keep on believing," I told him.

"So have you--uh--visited any other times?" he asked, changing the subject. "Seen anything historical?"

"Me? No. The time portal's pretty limited."

"And they haven't discovered life on other planets yet?" he asked.

"They thought they'd found evidence for microscopic life on Mars," I told him, "but that's still being debated. Some people think Europa, one of Jupiter's moons, might have life. It's got water ice and a thin atmosphere. They think there might be a huge water ocean under the shell of ice."

As we talked into the night, I felt some of the tension that had held me for so long seem to drain away. It was good to talk to him again. I remembered how much my brothers and I had enjoyed visiting him as children. He had always talked to us like adults, had taken what we said seriously and really listened. He was just as I had remembered. We talked until nearly one o'clock. Finally he showed me to the guest bedroom. I went to sleep feeling more secure, more content, than I had in months. I felt as if I had come home.

Chapter 5: School Days, School Days

"I don't suppose you'd care to come to school with me this morning," Mr. Delaney asked. He was frying up some bacon in a skillet. Coffee was brewing. I was sitting at the table feeling groggy.

"What would you tell the kids?"

"That you used to be one of my students," he said. "That you're in town visiting. You could be an aide. Frankly I could use one. Today's the last day of the year. The kids are going to be climbing the walls."

I thought about it. The chance to see Jaime, Larry, Jeff, myself, and all the others was more temptation than I could resist.

"You've got it," I said. "This is going to be good. By the way, my name in this time is John James Tarkington. That's what's on all my phony i.d. cards."

"Who's John James Tarkington?" Delaney asked.

"An ordinary college student about my age," I said. "One day he'll be the physicist who discovers the time distortions on Ghost Mountain."

"I see," he said. "I'll tell you what. To avoid confusing things, why don't we call you James Tarkington."

"Okay."

"Well, Dr. Tarkington," he said. "It'll be a pleasure to have an astrophysicist from NASA visiting my class."

* * *

The room smelled of ammonia-based floor polish, blackboard chalk, of books, formaldehyde, and of children. A life-sized skeleton, models of planets, and bottles of pickled snakes and animal innards sat in the class "museum" where they had for decades and soon wouldn't anymore.

Leonard Delaney called the homeroom roll for the last time. Young fresh faces looked back at him from their desks. Their pants legs were slightly flared at the bottom. Several of them were wearing tee shirts. One was wearing a Farrah Fawcett shirt. Two had shirts with Fonzie giving the thumbs-up signal. One little Trekkie--Jimmy Koslow, naturally--was wearing a blue *Star Trek* shirt with the black collar and the silver insignia on the upper chest. I had nearly laughed out loud when I saw him come in. He looked so intense.

"I was a handsome little guy," I whispered to Leonard. "I never would have thought it looking at those old school pictures."

A stranger, a long-haired phantom from another time, I sat at the back of the room and listened. The names had seemed like a forgotten song, like a familiar cadence heard every day for nearly nine months and stored somewhere in the subconscious mind. Some of the children I had forgotten completely. Others I remembered even though I hadn't thought about them in years.

Mr. Delaney was finishing up his bookkeeping when the door opened. Mr. Washburn, the principal, was there. Washburn was a portly black man in his early fifties. With him was a child.

"Mr. Delaney," Washburn said. "We have a new student."

Mr. Delaney looked up.

"On the last day?" he said.

"She just moved here with her mother," Washburn explained. "She wanted to meet the other children."

The girl was small with dark hair and ink-black eyes. She had only the humblest beginnings of the teen-age figure she had never grown up to possess. Even so, I had forgotten how strikingly beautiful she was. And she looked so tiny and so vulnerable. For a split-instant I saw her standing, carefree and innocent, between the rails of a train track. A locomotive was bearing down upon her with its single, unblinking eye fixed upon her in a hypnotic stare of death. I was scrambling up the tracks to pull her clear.

NO! GET OUT OF THERE! GET OUT OF THE WAY!

"Mr. Delaney," Washburn said. "This is Miss Jaime Mitchell."

Mr. Delaney jerked back like he'd been hit. He quickly buried his surprise and looked back at me. He cleared his throat and stood up.

"Nice to--uh--meet you," he said. He shook her small hand. "The children are about to change classes. You can sit back here until the bell rings." Completely forgetting about Washburn, he led her back to the desk behind Jimmy Koslow. My eleven-year-old counterpart was reading a *Swamp Thing* comic book. A cowlick on the crown of his head was standing straight up.

"Jim," Mr. Delaney said. Jim jerked up, afraid he was in trouble.

"Yes sir?"

"Jim," he said. "This is Jaime. She's visiting us today. They haven't placed her in a reading group yet. Could you show her to your classes?"

"Yes, sir," Jim said. He didn't look too enthusiastic. The other kids would make fun of him. They'd sing songs:

> *Jim and Jaime sitting in a tree*
> *K-I-S-S-I-N-G.*
> *First comes love, then comes marriage,*
> *Then comes Jim with a baby carriage.*

Jaime sat down behind him.

Jim went back to his comic book. Then Jaime started talking to him about comic books. Her older brother, it seemed, was an avid collector, and she liked to read them too. Then I--he--opened right up and started talking to her like we had been friends for years. She seemed to have a natural gift for charming people.

The bell rang. The children gathered their books and marched off to class. They were talking loudly.

"Hey!" Mr. Delaney shouted. "Hey! Let's have some order. I don't care if it is the last day of school."

They quieted down a little bit, but not much. As the room emptied out, Mr. Delaney made his way back to where I was standing.

"You could have warned me," he said.

"And miss that priceless look of surprise on your face?" I said.

"At my age, I could have had a priceless heart attack."

The roar of voices, footsteps, and lockers slamming poured through the door.

"How did you stand this all these years?" I asked.

"I've asked myself that same question every day for the past twenty years," he said.

Larry Christopher was in Mr. Delaney's first hour class. He crept in after everyone else was already sitting down. I had been looking forward to seeing him as a boy again, seeing my old friend through adult eyes. I watched him as he came in. He was such a skinny little kid. He was wearing a purple button-up shirt, brown corduroy pants and leather shoes. Most of the kids wore jeans, tee shirts, and tennis shoes. He wandered in, hardly looking up, and started for his desk. His eyes were far away.

Daryl, one of the bigger boys, stuck his foot out. Larry stumbled over it. He caught himself on the sink counter to his right, but spilled all of his books. The other children laughed. Larry, paying them little mind, bent over and gathered up his books.

"Hey!" I yelled. Both of them looked at me. "Put your books back down," I told Larry. Petrified, he obeyed. "Now," I told Daryl. "Pick up those books and give them to him."

He glared at me.

"Pick them up," I told him. "Now." We locked eyes in a battle of wills. Finally Daryl looked down, picked up the books, and shoved them into Larry's arms.

"Who are you anyway?" Daryl looked at me with dark, sullen eyes. In less than five years, those eyes would be peering out through prison bars.

Larry had made his way to his seat.

When the class was inside, Mr. Delaney had me cut off the lights. The projector screen was already pulled down behind him. He flipped on a movie projector and showed the class a super-eight millimeter filmstrip about the first voyage to the moon and another about the planets. Those took up most of the class period.

Two other groups passed through that morning before I saw Jaime and my younger self again. Then, at fourth hour, my group came in. I noticed several other *Star Trek* shirts in that group. I hadn't been as different as I had remembered. As with Jaime and Mr. Delaney, it felt weird to see Randy Gaines alive again. Randy had died in a freak accident during National Guard training.

Jaime came in behind Jim. She'd borrowed his *Swamp Thing* comic book and actually liked it. Some of the kids were already teasing him about her though. Martin Marvin, also known as "Martian," had started it. Martin was the smartest kid in the class, a bespectacled Einstein Junior. Martian could be a good friend sometimes. He had given Jim some of his old comic books. They had played in storm drains together during summer vacation. He could also be one of the meanest when it came to cutting remarks.

The group came in and sat down. Mr. Delaney handed them back their last test.

"Mr. Marvin," he said, holding out one of the papers. "I don't think this comment, 'Dinosaurs had small brains like Paul Hemphill,' was appropriate. That cost you five points on a perfect paper."

"I was kidding, Mr. Delaney."

"There's a time and place for everything, Martin," Mr. Delaney said, not unkindly. "Part of growing up is learning that."

I smiled to myself as he said it. I noticed my eleven-year-old counterpart was smiling too. Ours was the group Mr. Delaney always got stuck taking to lunch.

The last day meal was pizza, instant mashed potatoes, applesauce, and gingerbread. I sat with Mr. Delaney's class in the lunchroom. Some of the students asked me about where I was from, what kind of work I did, and so on. I told them that I lived in Houston, that I was a scientist. I'd have loved to tell them about working for NASA. That would have made me an instant celebrity, but it's hard for a celebrity to keep a low profile.

After lunch, they all went out for recess. Mr. Delaney had recess duty. I patrolled the playground with him.

"Haven't been out here in a while," I said. I looked around at the tetherballs on poles, at the monkey bars, and down the hill at the obstacle course where I had enjoyed playing when I was a kid. The course had chin-up bars, a tower with steps made of chain you used to climb it, and other wonders whose names I never heard--like the thing with the overhead rungs kids hang from with their hands and move from rung to rung.

At the edge of the course was a white wood fence. On the other side of this lay a shallow creek, a pine forest, and a creepy-looking old barn we used to tell ghost stories about. I watched from a distance as the kids got together to play. I remembered what had happened that day, and it was painful to watch.

The cosmic radiations of imagination swept down upon us and transformed us into the heroes of our dreams. We were once again ready to leap into our starships or fly unaided through the universe and destroy the forces of evil—almost. There was only one problem: what to do with Jaime.

"You can be Supergirl," I suggested. "She's got all the powers of Superman."

"Yeah," she said. "Super strength. X-ray vision."

"Why don't you go play with the girls?" Martian said. "You can go with her, Koslow. Maybe you can play doctor or something."

One of the other guys laughed a little nervously. Jim felt like they were all laughing at him. His face reddened.

"It's okay, Jim," Jaime said. "I'll see ya later." She started to leave.

"But . . . !" Jim started to say.

"I don't want you to get made fun of because of me," she said. "You can play with your friends, and I'll see you later." Jim watched silently as she walked away. I watched her go and felt myself starting to hurt.

"I should have stood up to Martian," I told Mr. Delaney. "I was such a wimp! I never should have let him do that to her."

"What are you talking about?" Delaney said.

"He wouldn't let Jaime play with us because she was a girl," I told him. "I should have at least gone with her, but it was my last day in sixth grade. In a way, I felt like it was the last day of my childhood--of the happiest part of my life. I wanted to spend it with my friends. Some friends."

"Well," Mr. Delaney said. "You're not doing anything right now are you?"

"That's true," I said. "That's very true."

I made my way slowly down to the obstacle course, trying not to look like I was going anywhere in particular.

Jaime hadn't gone to play with any of the other kids. She was playing by herself. She had found a big pine with low-hanging limbs and was climbing it. She was sitting on a branch about six feet up when I got to her.

"What are you doing up there?" I asked.

"Just looking around," she said. "I love to climb trees. My brother and me built a two-story tree house back where I used to live."

"Where'd you move here from?" I asked.

"Beaumont, Texas," she said. "My parents are getting divorced."

"I'm sorry to hear that," I said. "That's got to be hard on a person."

"It's not too bad," she said. "Mostly I miss my brother."

"He didn't come with you?" I asked.

"No," she said, standing up on the limb. "My dad had him from another marriage. He was just a half brother so my mom couldn't bring him. She wanted to, though."

I already knew this. Jaime's mother, Lisa, had married Donnie Mitchell while she was still in high school. Donnie ran a local restaurant. Lisa had worked for him. He had seemed, I guess, like a nice man at the time. Most alcoholics do when they're sober.

"You'd better be careful up there," I said. "You might fall and break something."

"My mom always says that," she said. "You better get down from there before you fall and break your neck."

"Growing up makes you paranoid," I told her.

"What does that mean?" she asked.

"Scared of everything that could happen," I told her.

"That's how my mom is," Jaime said. "Patranoid."

"Paranoid," I corrected. "But don't worry about it. It's just a side effect of loving kids."

"You're weird," Jaime said, smiling.

I stood and talked to her the rest of the break. Jaime seemed to have a gift for talking to people. There was something disarming about her way. You felt you could tell her anything, and she would understand. I knew she was probably that open with everyone she met, but I still wonder if she had sensed some part of her friend Jim in me--on an unconscious level, at least.

The bell rang.

"You'd better climb down from there and get back to class," I told Jaime.

"Help me down," she said.

"Sure."

She held onto the branch with her arms and legs and swung under it, getting ready to drop. I caught her by the waist and lowered her to the ground.

"Hi, Jim. Did you have a good time?"

I--the eleven-year-old me in the *Star Trek* shirt had just come back from a sweaty game of super hero role-playing.

"Not really," he said. "Our last day as kids and Martian had to ruin it." He looked depressed.

"Last day as kids?" I asked. "Why?"

"They don't play superheroes in junior high," he said miserably. "No space adventures. Nothing. You just stand around being bored all the time. That's what growing up is all about."

"Growing up isn't as bad as all that," I told him.

"I'm afraid he's right, Mr. James," Jaime said. "All my mom ever does is work."

"I'm sure she has fun sometime," I said.

"No," Jaime said. "Never."

I found Mr. Delaney and followed him back to the classroom where he was to teach the last class of his long career. The thirty restless, sweaty children could hardly bear to stay in their seats. Two of them nearly got in a fight as the filmstrip on planets was being shown. One had said something about the other one's mother.

The final bell signaled, for Leonard Delaney, the end of forty-three years in the classroom. He said his goodbyes and took the sweaty hugs and gentle handshakes of students he had taught and yelled at and loved and poured his life into.

When the last bus pulled away, the teachers were too weary to cheer—except for Mrs. Henry. She let out a victory yell and gave Mr. Delaney "five."

I stayed at the school until nearly six o'clock, helping Mr. Delaney load all of his books and classroom equipment into boxes. We neatly packed and labeled everything. Using a dolly he'd borrowed from Mr. Harris, the janitor, we filled the back of his El Camino truck with boxes.

"I'm leaving the rest of this here for the new science teacher," he finally said. "I remember how I didn't have anything when I first started out."

He looked around the room for a long time.

"I guess that's it," he said. "I just can't believe I won't be coming back next year."

After we had walked out, he took out a key and locked the door behind us. The other teachers had long since gone home.

"You like seafood?" he asked as we were locking up. "There's a place on the lake that serves the best fish, steak, oysters, shrimp . . ."

"Sounds good," I said.

We walked out to his El Camino. He turned the key, revved up the engine, and shoved an eight-track tape into the tape deck.

"You like Neil Diamond?" he asked.

"Sweet Caroline all the way."

"You're a good man." The music started. He put the truck into first gear, and we rolled away. "I just can't believe I won't be coming back next year."

* * *

That night I found myself sitting in the dark at Leonard's table drinking decaf coffee and thinking. I was wrestling with phantom thoughts.

"Pretty much ended life for her mama, though," Dad had said.

"I'm afraid Jaime's mother was just sorry anyway," Mom's voice echoed. *"Last I heard, she and her live-in boyfriend had been arrested for selling dope. No telling what Jaime would have gone through if she had lived."*

I thought about the parables I had heard in my childhood. The phantoms of Frankenstein's monster and a shriveled monkey's paw from a Somerset Maughm story crawled across my mind.

"Got any more of that coffee?" Leonard asked. He flipped on the light over the stove.

"Couldn't sleep either, huh?" I asked.

"I don't seem to sleep as much now that I'm older," he said. "Instant decaf, huh?" He filled a kettle with water and turned on a stove burner.

"I didn't tell you everything about Jaime," I told him.

"What about her?" he asked.

"It's her home life," I told him. "She was running away from home on the night of the accident. She said she couldn't live with her mother anymore. She'd written a note, packed her suitcase, and was on her way to Texas. After Jaime died, her mother got into drugs and everything else."

He nodded, pulled up a chair, and sat down next to me.

"So you're having second thoughts about saving her life?" Leonard asked me.

"No," I said. "I just wonder if saving her life is enough. What if I'm condemning her to a living hell by saving her? Or what if she turns out just like her mother?"

"I wish I knew what to tell you," he said. "You're a time traveler, but you're not God."

"No," I said. "But I've spent a lot of time talking to Him lately."

Chapter 6: Jinx

The first day of summer vacation that year was one of those days you remember forever. A cool front had come through. The heat and humidity of an Arkansas June were held at bay for a few days as the air currents battled it out overhead. There were only a few clouds in the sky. While I was relaxing at Leonard Delaney's house, my twelve-year-old counterpart was already exploring the world.

Jim was hardly even sweating when he pushed his bike under a fence and up a hill and came out on the corner of Payne and Willow. This was a neighborhood of small but neatly kept homes with mowed yards.

He pulled his bike into a narrow dirt alleyway that separated the back yards of houses that stood back-to-back with each other as they faced two adjacent streets.

The third back yard to the right was shaded by young pine trees. In that yard was a small garden, a muddy duck pond, a wooden tower, and a small, white clubhouse made of wood and painted cardboard. A hammering noise was coming from inside.

Jim strained to look through the window. He could see someone inside, a slender figure hammering away on something. He waited, watching the clubhouse.

The figure inside looked up. He ducked and came out of the door and around the side. Larry Christopher smiled.

"What are you doing?" Jim asked.

"Working on an invention," Larry said.

After he'd helped Jim get his bike over the fence, Larry brought Jim into his clubhouse and showed him all of his latest work. The inside of the clubhouse was cramped. It had been built for smaller kids. A small plywood table was piled with the instruments of science--a chemistry set, wire cutters, some black tape, some erector set pieces, a microscope, and the inventions.

Larry had a nude G.I. Joe-type action doll sliced up and filled with wires and circuit boards. A miniature android, he was. He didn't do anything, but he did look neat. Next to that was a grappling hook Larry was making from a bent spike. That was what he had been hammering on. Finally, Larry was using his chemistry set to try to brew a super strength formula from vitamin supplements and various household chemicals. No success so far.

Jim told Larry about his birthday party the following afternoon. Larry said he would try to come. They talked of robots and inventions for a time.

"What do you want to do?" Larry finally asked Jim after he had showed him everything.

"Let's go up to the wax museum," Jim said. "We can look around up there."

"I thought it was burned down," Larry said.

"It's just partway burned down," Jim said. "You can still go in. We'll need a flashlight though."

"That's okay. I've got one."

"Let's go to the E-Z Stop first and get some Icees and stuff so we can have a picnic."

They rode through the neighborhood, came out of an alley behind the E-Z Stop, pulled their bikes around front, and knocked the kickstands into place. They stepped inside. The bell on the door jingled as they came in.

Jim walked straight to the comic book rack.

"Heeeey!" somebody said. The voice sounded delighted.

Jim and Larry turned around. Jaime Mitchell was strolling up to them looking like she hadn't been so happy to see someone in her life.

"Hey, Jaime," Jim said, a little embarrassed to see her. He remembered something about introducing people he had learned in language class. "Jaime, this is Larry. Larry, this is Jaime."

Larry looked at her a little warily. He didn't trust people easily.

"Whatcha doin'?" Jaime asked.

"We're going bike riding," Jim said. "Stopped here to pick up a few supplies. We're going to the wax museum."

"Can I come?" Jaime asked. "Please. I don't have nothing to do. It's so boring around here."

Jim and Larry looked at each other.

"Okay," they said, a little bit reluctant. Jaime followed them as they did the rest of their shopping.

Between the two of them, Jim and Larry purchased two comic books, two mixed Coke and Lemon-Lime swirled Icees, two sticks of beef jerky, and a box of chocolate fudge Pop-Tarts. The woman behind the counter smiled as she rang it up. She was an attractive woman--brown eyed, brown haired--but she was puffing on a cigarette, a nasty-looking old cigarette with the ash hanging down. Jim hated it when women smoked. It was something the bad kids did on the A&P parking lot Friday night. Of course their cigarettes weren't always just tobacco either.

Jaime walked around behind the counter.

"Mama," she said. "Can I go bike riding with Jim and Larry?"

So this woman, Jim and Larry realized, was Jaime's mother.

"Where are they going?" Mrs. Mitchell asked.

"To the wax museum. Can I go?"

"Does it cost anything?" she asked.

"No," Jim said. He didn't want to mention that they would be trespassing in an abandoned building. Jaime's mom looked suspicious.

"How far away is it?" she asked. Jaime looked at Jim and Larry for the answer.

"About two miles," Larry said. He never could judge distances very well. It was closer to eight. I couldn't remember either, so I didn't say anything.

"Okay," Mrs. Mitchell finally said after a few more protests and questions. "But come right back."

"Okay," Jaime said.

Jim, Larry, and Jaime left the store together.

"I need to get my bike," Jaime said.

"Do you live close to here?" Jim said.

"A few streets over," Jaime said. "Can you ride me on the back of your bike?"

"Okay," Jim said as he threw his leg over and placed his foot on the pedal.

She climbed on behind him and put her arms around him. She was so soft and she smelled like perfume--or was it wild cherry Lifesavers? Jim felt his face getting red. Larry didn't seem to notice.

"Let's go," he said.

They pulled onto the sidewalk and started toward Jaime's house. The sidewalk went downhill, so Jim didn't have too much trouble getting started with Jaime on the back. The sky was looking overcast now. There weren't any shadows.

Jaime lived in a trailer park. Her bike, she said, was inside the rusty metal shed next to her mother's well-worn trailer home. The door of the shed was chained shut with a combination lock. Jaime dialed the combination right the first time, tugged on the lock, and it opened. She unstrung the chain and swung open a rickety tin door. Inside the shed was a lawn mower, a gas can, a mildewed ice chest, and a beat-up red bicycle with worn coaster brake cables and rips in the seat. Jaime rolled the bike out into daylight, propped it against the trailer, and closed the door of the shed. She squeezed the lock shut.

"That's a boy's bike," Jim said. Instantly he was sorry he had said it.

"No, it's not," Jaime said. "It's my bike. It did used to belong to my brother though. He gave it to me."

"Does he live here?" Jim asked.

"No," Jaime said. "He still lives with my dad. He's really my half brother. I miss him sometimes." She changed the subject. "Let me run inside and get something."

She pulled a key out of her pocket, unlocked the door of the trailer, and went inside. Jim and Larry looked at each other, sighed, and waited. She came back in about two minutes with a metal lunch box. It had motorcycle riders painted on the front and sides. She put it in a basket on the back of her bike.

* * *

I was sitting in a folding chair on the front porch of Hassle Johnson's Country Store drinking A&W Root Beer from a bottle.

A dark armada of thunderheads had converged over the mountain highway that ran past the store and on to infinity. I saw a flash somewhere over one of the mountains. An artillery burst of thunder tumbled down across the sky. I looked at my watch. Rain peppered the road, the parking lot, and the grass. Everything smelled sweet. Yes, it was just about time.

I put on my helmet, climbed on my motorcycle, kick-started it, turned around, and pulled back out onto the highway. The road was slick. I felt the bike slide sideways under me. Finally the tire grabbed and the bike moved forward. My heart was hammering in my chest as I moved along.

Stupid, stupid, stupid! It would be just perfect for me to crash my bike back in the past and end up just like Anderson and Jaime.

I rode through a shimmering curtain of water. It collected on me as I passed. I felt it running across my hands. I passed a billboard on the side of a mountain:

DR. CAULDER'S HOUSE OF WAX. 1 1/2 MILES.

I zipped over a bridge and rounded a hairpin turn in the road. By that time I could see something in the road ahead of me, three ink-black shapes shimmying from side to side.

I pulled ahead of them, stopped, killed the engine, and raised the visor of my helmet.

Jim Koslow, Jaime Mitchell, and Larry Christopher were all soaking wet. Their hair was plastered to their smooth, preteen foreheads. Their clothes were dark with water. They had been laughing. Now they eyed me warily.

"I know you," Jim finally said. "You were at school."

"Yeah," Jaime said. "You were the duty teacher."

"What are you kids doing out in this rain?" I asked them.

"Going to the wax museum," Jim said. "Larry said it wasn't but two miles. We've been going about ten."

Larry still hadn't said anything.

"Do you know how far it is?" Jaime asked me.

"It's just ahead," I told them. "You're almost there. Follow me."

I led them in the last leg-wringing half mile. We all topped a hill, rounded a corner, and found ourselves rolling past the face of a grim, Victorian-looking building. A long, frowning porch ran across the front. A turret on the side came to a steeple-like point. One side of the building had been scorched by fire.

"That's it," Larry said.

I braked, swung from the saddle of my cycle, and killed the engine. I pulled the bike up next to the porch, underneath the eaves of the roof, and put down the kickstand. Jim, Jaime, and Larry pulled their bikes up onto the porch. It creaked beneath them. They had been laughing when I first saw them, enjoying the rain. Now they just looked cold.

The windows across the front of the house were covered by sheets of plywood. Dirty words and names were carved in them or written in spray paint. The front door had been nailed shut, but the bottom panel had been knocked out. Pieces of splintered wood hung there.

"Are we gonna go in?" I asked, but I heard another voice saying it too. Then I realized little Jim had just asked the same thing.

"Jinx!" Jaime said.

"What?" I asked.

"Jinx," Jaime said. "It's a game. When two people say the same thing, you say, 'Jinx.'"

"Let's bring the food," Larry said quietly, still wary of me. "I've got some matches too."

"Leave the matches," I said. "This place is a fire trap. Don't any of you ever start a fire in here."

"You're being paranoid again," Jaime told me.

Larry didn't say anything. He got down on his hands and knees and looked through the ruined door. Then he stood up, walked over to his bike, and started going through the little pouch he had hanging on a bar beneath the seat. He brought out a battery-powered flashlight. He didn't say anything, but a smug grin pulled at the corners of his mouth.

"He's got everything in that bike bag," Jim told Jaime. "He's got Band-Aids, a tool kit, tire repair stuff."

"Just like Batman," I said. "Batrope, batarang, bat laser gun, bat gas pellets, bat fingerprint kit, batlight." I got a light of my own out of the pack on the back of my motorcycle.

Larry had crawled through the bottom part of the door.

"Come on."

His faint call sounded like the voice of a ghost.

Feeling guilty about trespassing, but too curious not to go on, Jim crawled in. He was carrying the bag with the Pop Tarts and beef jerky. Jaime followed him with her lunch box.

I was almost trembling with anticipation. The day we had all gone to the wax museum was one of those childhood memories that you hang onto and treasure. I can't count the number of times I've dreamed about the wax museum since then.

I got down and crawled through behind the kids. Larry was already shining his flashlight around. In front of us was a burned-out staircase. Everything was smoke stained. Larry's flashlight brushed across something on the floor.

"Wait! Wait!" Jim yelled. "What's that?"

It was a partly-melted wax figure of a man in nineteenth century clothes--a big waistcoat and watch.

"Must be Dr. Caulder," I said.

They looked at me blankly.

"Oh, yeah," Jim finally said. "Dr. Caulder's House of Wax."

"This place is creepy," Jaime said.

To the left of the stairway was the part of the museum hit hardest by the fire. Nothing was left but heaps of blackened rubble. Miraculously the outer walls of the building had been left standing, but the inside was nothing but debris--charred wood, a few headless *papier mache'* bodies, and some ruined furniture. Lonely spokes of daylight filtered through the rafters overhead. Rain dripped down through the roof and onto the scorched wood and heaps of cinder.

"Not much left here," Jim and I said at the same time. We looked at each other with amusement.

"Jinx!" Jaime said again.

Larry had turned his light around the other way. He walked past the stairs, around the charred figure on the floor, and toward a dark hallway with moldy carpet on the floor.

"Did you ever go through here when the museum was open?" Jim asked Larry.

"Yeah," Larry said. "Two times." That was all.

We followed Larry down the dreary hallway. Something brushed across Jim's hand. He yelled and jumped back against a wall. Jaime screamed.

"What is it? What is it?" Larry yelled, swinging his light around.

"Something touched my hand," Jim said.

Larry and I probed the hall with our lights. Our circles of light converged on a dust-covered plastic palm tree in a pot of dirt. We all laughed.

The hallway ended in an arch painted to look like gray stone. Larry and I flashed our lights around. There were gas lamps embedded head-high on either side of the arch.

We stepped through into a street, a narrow cobblestone street from nineteenth century London. Gas lamps lined the walk at even intervals. A bobby with a tall helmet and a nightstick walked his beat. Someone had broken off one of his arms and pulled off half of his moustache. Three men in tall hats, long coats, lambchop sideburns, and scarves huddled together over a hymnbook and sang silent carols in front of a shop. "Scrooge and Marley" a label in the window said. Somebody had sprayed an obscenity below that in spray paint. Between that building and the next one was an alley. Jack the Ripper was standing with his back against the wall with a medical bag in one hand and a surgical knife in the other.

"He looks real," Jim said, looking at the twisted, evil face. "If he so much as twitches, I'm going through these walls."

The others agreed.

I shined my light around to other shop windows.

Stone steps led up to a porch with a shingle hanging from it. "Sherlock Holmes," the sign said. The house next door had a sign proclaiming its owner to be a Dr. Henry Jekyll.

"This is like one of those old movies," Jim said, his voice hushed with awe. "This is cool, Larry. I'm glad we came here."

To their left, the shops had been replaced by a tall stone wall with barbed points along the top. Artificial tree limbs hung over it. A black horse-drawn carriage blocked the road ahead of them. The driver wore a tall hat, a scarf, a waistcoat, and gloves with holes for the fingers. The horse was a real horse even though it had been stuffed. Fur was coming off in places.

"I wonder if they killed this horse just to make this," Jaime said. "That would be terrible."

"Maybe he died of old age," Jim said.

"I think it's an artificial horse," I told them. "Looks real though."

Since the road ahead of us was blocked, the only way to go was left through an arched wrought-iron gateway in the fence.

Artificial trees crowded in on both sides of the path. I walked ahead of my preteen friends. Jaime got between Jim and Larry and held onto their arms. Beneath a street lamp, beside a park bench, Sherlock Holmes and Dr. Watson were kneeling over a woman's body. Holmes was wearing his coat and hat, smoking his pipe, and holding up his magnifying glass. His arms were bent in slightly unnatural positions. Someone had partially undressed the female dummy they were kneeling over, but she was about as anatomically detailed as your average Barbie doll.

"I wonder who took her clothes off," Jaime said. "And wrote all of those dirty words on everything."

"Probably a bunch of teenagers smoking dope," Jim said. That had been Dad's stock explanation for most of the bizarre behavior we heard about.

"You're probably right," I smiled.

"Come on," Larry said. "You've got to see some of this other stuff."

Mr. Hyde was crouched in the shadows behind a tree. His twisted features were almost hidden by the cloak he held up with one arm. With his other arm, he waved a walking stick.

We came to a painted-stone wall and walked through a door. We found ourselves in a cozy room with red carpet and a fireplace. In a chair, Ebenezer Scrooge was reeling back from the rotting, skeletal specter of Jacob Marley.

"I love this story," Jim said. "I watch it every Christmas as many times as I can."

"Me, too," Jaime said. "I like the old black and white ones."

Marley's ponderous chains, weights, and boxes of money dragged the floor. His face was contorted in silent anguish.

Scrooge, dressed in a nightshirt and cap, was about to spill his bowl of gruel. The Scrooge figure looked more cartoonish than real. The nose was a bit too long and the fear too exaggerated.

At one end of the room was a row of stairs.

As Jim, Jaime, Larry, and I moved up the stairs, we passed different scenes from Scrooge's life. In one setting, the weary old man and a young woman in flowing robes stood behind a park bench on which a young man and woman were sitting. The trees were bare. There was snow on the ground. The young woman wore a long dress, gloves, and a bonnet. She looked sad.

"That's Scrooge and his girlfriend," Jim narrated.

"No," Larry said. "Scrooge is standing back there."

"He's seeing himself," Jim said. "Didn't you ever see that movie?"

In the next scene, Scrooge--still in nightclothes--and a hefty bearded giant in a long, kingly robe are standing on a street corner watching as Bob Cratchett lifts Tiny Tim up to his shoulder. Tim waves his crutch in the air.

As we reached a landing and started up another flight of stairs, Scrooge lay in a graveyard, recoiling in terror from his own tombstone. A fleshless shape in a rotting cowl and robe pointed sternly at the stone, its face a shadowed mystery as the future itself is.

"That's the Ghost of Christmas Future," Jaime said. "He's always the scariest looking ghost. I saw one movie where he had a sheet over his head."

"I saw that one," Larry said. "You could see through it when the light hit him right."

We went a few steps higher. Scrooge was standing at the top of the stairs with the Cratchett family. Tiny Tim was sitting on his shoulder and everyone looked happy.

Walking down a hall, we passed H.G. Wells sitting in a time machine, a wild-looking contraption of whirling dials, spinning wheels, and copper tubing. As I was absorbing the symbolism of Wells' vision of time travel, we passed Dr. Frankenstein who was about to inject some unholy serum into the hulking body of his creation, still lifeless on a slab. The metaphor of science gone too far seemed to shake a finger of warning at me.

We watched Captain Ahab stand on his peg leg and curse as he threw his harpoon into the looming white specter of Moby Dick. The seamen with him screamed as their craft began to capsize. Waves of glistening plastic foamed up from beneath the boat.

"This is what happens when you let yourself be controlled by your obsessions," Ahab seemed to say to me. Suddenly it seemed that every display we passed was a metaphoric warning directed at unwary time travelers.

Jim, Jaime, Larry, and I crept past the Phantom of the Opera. The disfigured opera singer was playing wildly away on a big organ. I couldn't find any symbolism there, thank goodness.

An arrow pointed into a little alcove with stairs leading upward. "To the Tower," a sign said.

I led the way up the stairs. The walls and stairs were all painted gray. The stairs came out in an open, circular room full of gargoyles. A big, metal bell stood in the middle of the room. Clinging to it was the thick, twisted body of the Hunchback of Notre Dame. He didn't really look all that mean or scary, just sad. Windows of stained glass circled the room, letting in light from the outside world. There were flashes of lightning. Thunder groaned. Rain swept against the glass.

We left the tower, went back down to the lower level, and continued down the hall. The corridor looped back around and we found ourselves on a darkened balcony overlooking nineteenth-century London. Larry and I swept the chasm below with our feeble electric torches. We could see the street, the buildings, and the grim wonders of the park. This balcony overlooked the place we had been before. Shining the light higher, we saw figures of Peter Pan, Wendy, and the other children--all suspended by wires--flying toward an image of St. Stephen's Tower, the site of Big Ben.

"I wish we could have seen this place all lit up," Jim said. "It must have been great."

"It was," Larry said. He sighed and sat down with his back against the wall, still shining his light out onto painted London buildings.

"Let's have a picnic," he said.

Jim and Jaime sat down in the floor. Larry held his light up as Jim opened his bag and dug out his comic book, Pop Tarts, and beef jerky. Jaime opened her lunch box and pulled out an apple, some crackers, and a Thermos jug full of juice.

"You can have some of my Pop Tarts," Jim told me.

"That's generous of you," I said.

We ate and talked as the thunder groaned somewhere far distant.

"You guys have got to come to my birthday party," Jim said.

"When is it?" Jaime asked.

"Tomorrow," Larry said, chewing on a Pop Tart. "Can I ride with you?" she asked.

"If my mother will take me," Larry said. "I haven't asked her yet."

When their stomachs were filled, they huddled their soggy bodies together--Jaime in the middle--and read comic books in the glow of Larry's flashlight. I scanned the area around us with my flashlight.

Huddled against Jaime's side, Jim could almost imagine what it would be like to put his arm around her, to hold her. She was so close, and so perfect. What was a guy supposed to do?

After a long time, they stood up, and we took one last look around.

"I'm gonna have to come back here with a camera," Jim said. They all agreed it was a good idea.

We walked a little further down the corridor, turned a corner, and found ourselves staring--squinty-eyed--into daylight and falling rain. About twelve feet from them, the corridor ended. Blackened pieces of wood hung down. The floor under their feet became rickety. Beneath the carpet, they could feel the floorboards starting to buckle. Loud squeaks came with every step.

"This is where everything burned," Jim said. "We better not go any further. We might fall through."

Larry and Jaime kept walking, almost to the edge of the chasm.

"You're gonna fall!" Jim warned them.

"It's okay," Jaime said.

"It should be all right," I told them, "but be careful."

Jim edged closer to the abyss. About ten feet below them, heaps of blackened wood, carpet, burned cloth, and ruined figures of charred *papier mache'* and melted wax lay spread like some

World War II holocaust. The outer walls still stood. Part of the roof had held, but it was slowly caving in. Walls and bits of the floors of some of the adjacent rooms and corridors were intact, but the damage was heavy.

"How did this happen?" Jaime asked.

"Bad wiring was what I heard," Jim said. "But some people think the owner burned it down to get the insurance money. There weren't many customers way out here."

"I wish it hadn't burned," Jaime said. "It's such a cool place. You wonder what the rest of it was like."

"They had some of the presidents and kings," Larry said. "And Ichabod Crane being chased through Sleepy Hollow by the Headless Horseman. And they had some of the old actors like Clark Gable."

We walked back through the museum. We passed the balcony, the scenes from Scrooge's life, the park, and the London street. Finally we were back in the room with the burned figure and the stairs.

"I wonder what's up these stairs," Jim said.

Jim, Larry, Jaime, and I climbed the smoky stairs up into darkness. We passed a room of stone. Sitting on the floor around a low table, Jesus, Peter, John, and the rest enjoyed their last meal together. A gritty-looking chunk of unleavened bread, some clay flasks, and a platter of lamb's meat were spread out amid some candle stumps. Jesus held up the bread and cup to the others.

"He looks so real," Jim said. "They all do."

"I wish He was real," Jaime said. "Maybe He could tell my parents to get back together. Maybe they would listen to Him."

"Do you think they would?" I asked her. "Listen, I mean."

She sighed.

"Prob'ly not," she said. She squeezed up against my side, and I put my arm around her for a moment.

I spent the whole afternoon with those children. I had felt weird about fate, genetics, and personality every Jaime said *jinx*. Jim and I chorused each other seven times in all. After all those years, I thought I had changed, and I had! But there was some basic essence in the make-up of James Koslow that would always be the same, it seemed.

To only be eleven, my young twin took life seriously.

"I wish we could all be like this forever," he said. "But someday we'll all grow up and go to different places. We might not even remember each other anymore. It'll be like we're not even the same people."

"I used to worry about that," I told him. "But I guarantee you we will still be the same people. There's some part of you that never really changes. You can lose sight of it for a while. You may cover it up with games. But it's still there. It never completely goes away." I wanted to tell him Larry and I were still friends and that my love for Jaime had brought me back through time to save her, but I couldn't say that.

Jim, Larry, and Jaime climbed onto their bicycles and pedaled back around the edge of the museum. I kick-started my motorcycle and followed them. I rode with them for a while, slowing down and letting them get ahead, then catching up.

Finally we said our goodbyes, and I took off through the gray toward town. As I was shooting past the post office, I passed a big, copper-colored Rambler. The woman driving looked like she had been crying. It was Lisa Mitchell.

I gritted my teeth and shivered inwardly. I knew what was coming.

You're never going anywhere with them again.

I hate that woman. No wonder Jaime's dad divorced her.

I remembered my own words as clearly as if I had just spoken them. Something inside of me flinched at the sound of the hate in my own young voice. In my mind, I could see Lisa Mitchell's tear-streaked face, the face of a frightened young woman. I couldn't hate her now. I hoped I had been wrong about her. I hoped, but I didn't know--and I did want to know. I rode back to Leonard's house in the gray and found Leonard asleep in front of the television set.

Chapter 7: Happy Birthday to Me

I woke up gasping for breath. I barely remembered the dream I'd just escaped from. I was gridlocked in traffic in some dark and nameless city, and I couldn't find an off ramp. I had to get to Jaime, but the cars wouldn't move. They were jammed together so tightly, I couldn't even get the door of my car open to run away on foot.

I've failed. That's what I was thinking. I've come all the way back in time, and I've gotten myself trapped in a traffic jam.

"An accident on Highway 75 north of Miracle Springs has claimed the lives of a twelve-year-old female and an unidentified male," a radio announcer was saying. He went on.

Too late. I was too late.

That was when I woke up. Reality settled in around me. The sense of sweating claustrophobia left me slowly. Leonard Delaney's house. The guest room. Early Saturday morning.

I wasn't too late. This was the day, and I wasn't too late.

I went back to sleep and dreamed I'd slept through the whole day. Mr. Delaney came in and told me paramedics had recovered Jaime's body from the base of the cliff.

"You should have set the alarm clock," he said accusingly.

After waking up the second time, I got up early, went into the den, and flipped on the television set. I had to do something to get my mind off the task that awaited me. Saturday morning cartoons were showing. For the first time in ages, I watched *Scooby Doo, Shazam, Land of the Lost,* and some of my other old favorites.

Leonard was preparing lunch when the phone rang. I wondered if I should answer it. Then I heard Leonard walking across the kitchen. He picked up the phone. I could hear him talking, but couldn't make out the words. A few seconds later, he walked into the den.

"We've just been invited to your birthday party," he said.

At four-thirty I had showered and put on a fresh change of clothes for my twelfth birthday party. As I watched my parents' house getting closer and closer I realized how much I had been fighting back the urge to go running back to the home I'd grown up in, knock on my parents' door, and tell them I wanted to look all through their house and yard. I felt my body tensing with anticipation.

Leonard parked the truck in the driveway behind my dad's Buick and killed the engine. The garage was on the side of the house. My family was in the back yard. The grass was freshly cut. It was a bright, early spring color of green. Dad was grilling steaks. Mom was setting the table--putting ice in the glasses, laying out silverware, and so on. Again I was struck by how young and attractive my folks looked. They were only a few years older than I was.

Jim and Jaime were playing against Larry and Jason in a game of badminton. Barry was playing with Cindy, our Boston Terrier.

"It's like walking into a home movie," I said as I was opening the door. It was true.

Dad flipped a steak over and started over to us. Mom stopped working at the table and came with him.

"Glad you could make it," my dad told Leonard. They shook hands.

"Jim enjoyed your class so much this year," Mom said. "He came home every evening talking about what he had learned in class that day."

"He's a good student," Leonard said. "Eager to learn. I wish I'd had more like him over the years." Then he turned to me. "This is James Tarkington. I taught him when he was Jim's age. He's staying with me for a few days."

"Ed Koslow," my dad introduced himself to me. We shook hands. Naturally my parents would treat me like a stranger, but I hadn't really prepared myself for it. It gave me an empty feeling. I felt more cut off now than I had when the helicopter had first left me in the woods that evening.

"Were you the one who took the kids through the wax museum?" my mother asked.

"Well," I said, afraid of getting into trouble, "They were almost there and pretty soaked when I found them. We walked through it together while we were waiting for the rain to stop"

"Thanks for watching after them," she said. "I didn't know they were going all the way up there. I told Jim not to go back. I'm afraid the whole thing's going to fall in one day."

Leonard walked back to the truck and lifted the box out of the bed. I was carrying my gift in a brown grocery sack.

"What have you got there?" my dad asked Leonard.

"A birthday present," he said.

"You didn't have to do that, Leonard," my dad said.

"I know," he said. "But birthdays are such a big thing when you're his age. I stopped having them a long time ago, but when you're twelve. . . Well, that's a different thing."

We walked over to the card tables my mother had set up. She had Tupperware bowls of potato salad and baked beans there. My birthday cake, done in the shape of a rocket ship, was there on the table. The candles hadn't been lit.

I remember that cake, I thought. Heck, I remember those aluminum drinking glasses we used to have, too.

"Hi, Mr. Delaney," Jim said. "Hi, James." He was still swatting at the birdie.

"How's it going?" I said.

"Hi, Mr. Delaney," Jaime said. "Hi, James."

"Hi, Mr. Delaney."

"Whose serve?" Jason asked.

"Ours," Jaime said.

I noticed Mom had picked up her box camera and was shooting movies of the evening. I turned my head to keep her from getting a clear shot of me.

"The steaks are ready," my dad said, lifting them from the grill with a spatula.

"You kids need to finish your game up later," Mom said. "It's time to eat."

They put the rackets down against the poles, got paper plates from a stack on one of the tables, and seated themselves.

"Would you return thanks for us, Leonard?" my dad asked.

Leonard led the prayer, and everything grew quiet. He said, "Amen," and the bustle of children returned. We passed around the meat, potato salad, and beans. My mother had also baked some homemade rolls.

After supper was gone, my mother took the plastic wrap off the pan where the birthday cake was. My mother had etched a space ship in the icing. Dad lit the candles. Mom got out the camera and filmed Jim as he blew them all out.

"What did you wish for?" Jason asked.

"He wants to marry Jaime," Barry mocked.

"Shut up," Jim said. *How did he know what I wished for?*

Barry stuck his tongue out, potato salad still sitting on it. I strangled on a mouthful of tea. Everyone looked at me.

"Sorry."

After we had finished most of the cake, a bag of colorfully wrapped boxes was brought out. I tried to remember what I had gotten that year. As Jim unwrapped his gifts, it all seemed familiar to me: models of a *Star Trek* shuttlecraft and of *the Six Million Dollar Man* kicking in a door, a Panasonic tape recorder, and a stack of comic books.

"Open Mr. Delaney's present," Barry said.

"What present?" Jim asked. Leonard had put the box on the ground beside him. Now he picked it up and passed it to Jim. Jim took the box carefully, opened the lid and looked inside. His eyes widened.

"You're giving me this?" he asked.

"Yeah," Leonard said. "I wanted you to have it."

Inside the box were a flaming red model rocket with a skull and cross bones on the side, a launch pad, and a remote control box with wires sticking out of it.

"What is it?" Jaime asked.

"It's his model rocket," Jason said. "The one he launched at school. Isn't it, Jim?"

"Yeah," Jim said. "And the launcher and everything."

"You sure you want to part with that, Leonard?" my dad asked.

"Yeah," he said. "My science teaching days are over. Jim, here, has more use for it than me. And now that he's got the launcher, he can build himself some other rockets too."

"Wow," Jim said. "I can't believe you really gave me your rocket, Mr. Delaney."

"Can we fly it?" Jason asked. He looked at Mr. Delaney.

"It's Jim's stuff," he shrugged. "What about it, Jim?"

"Can we use your mower, dad?" Jim asked. "It's got to be wired to a battery."

Dad walked back to the old tin storage barn we had in our back yard.

"I'm sorry I didn't bring you anything," Jaime said. She was feeling pretty bad about it. I could tell.

"That's all right," Jim said, thinking nothing of it.

"You couldn't have brought anything that would have made him any happier anyway," I told her. "I think he's just glad *you* could come."

"I was going to get him a model of Mr. Spock shooting a laser gun at a snake," she explained. "They've got one at Ben Franklin's, but my mom said I was grounded because I stayed at the wax museum too long."

"But she still let you come today?" I asked.

"Well," she said. "I was going to ask her before she went to work, but I forgot." She grinned sheepishly.

"Okay," Jim said. "Let's launch the rocket."

* * *

Leonard and I helped my parents bring the food, dishes, and eating utensils back inside while the children played. Overwhelmed by nostalgia, I looked around the kitchen and den to see how things looked. Barry had left his stuffed monkey lying on the couch. Jim's record album of the Orson Welles *War of the Worlds* radio broadcast was lying on top of the stereo cabinet next to a stack of John Denver albums. The curtains were a different color.

"Thanks for helping clean up, James," my mother said. "And thanks for saying that about the comic books." Dad and I had had a conversation about the educational value of comics after the rocket launch. I'd given them credit for my success in graduate school. "Ed and Jim have been arguing over that for the longest time. Jim loves them. Ed thinks they're a waste of money." She and I were the only ones in the house at that moment. The others were out back.

"I remember how it was," I told her. "My dad wanted me to grow up so fast--to go from being a kid to an adult all in one fell swoop."

"Ed's afraid the other kids will laugh at Jim," she said. "He doesn't want him to be different."

"He's got to be himself," I told her. "Even if some people do laugh. I used to get picked on by the guys in gym class because I did too well in school and went to church. Go figure!"

Mom didn't say anything. She was looking at me with this strange, haunted expression. I was afraid I'd made her mad at first. Then the truth came to me: she had recognized me.

"I'm sorry if I overstepped my bounds," I said.

"No," she said. "It's not that. It's something else."

Just then the door opened, and my younger counterpart walked in.

"James," he said. "You want to see my room?"

"You bet," I said.

"He may not have time," my mother said.

"I wouldn't miss this for the world," I told her.

He led me up the stairs. I felt my heart beating faster. The bathroom was right at the top. My old bedroom was directly to the left of the bathroom. The door was ajar.

Jim pushed open the door, walked in, and switched on the lights. I stepped in behind him into a trove of wonders. My bedspread had leopards on it. To the right of the bed was a bookcase where I had stacked all of the books I had ordered from the book order forms the teacher used to pass out.

The walls were covered with posters of old friends. Apes from *The Planet of the Apes*, Fonzie, Elvis, Steve Austin, Jaime Sommers, the Hardy Boys, Nancy Drew, and Jacklyn Smith were all taped to the walls.

"Quite an art gallery you've got here," I said.

"Yeah," Jim said. "I got most of 'em out of *Dynamite* magazine."

"Oh, yeah," I said. "Those were--are great."

I noticed a map of Six Flags Over Texas mounted on the wall too. I looked at the map, at the Rotoriculus, the Spelunker's Cave, the Big Bend, and LaSalle's Riverboat Ride. None of those rides were there anymore.

"Here's all my comic books," Jim said, opening his closet door. On the floor were two big cardboard boxes overflowing with comic books. To one side, underneath the clothes, I noticed a toy box. G.I. Joe, the Hulk, Evel Knieval, Mr. Spock, Steve Austin, Jaime Sommers, Batman, and a host of other favorites lay in twisted positions beneath the raised lid. They looked like they were trying to force their way out.

"That's quite a toy collection you've got there," I said. "How's it going, guys?" I whispered to Hulk, Evel, and the rest. Jim went through the box, showing me all of his favorites. The other kids came in. We took some of the old Evel Knieval stunt bikes to the stairs and jumped them off for old times' sake. Leonard and my parents walked in as we were launching the Canyon Sky Cycle.

"There you are," Leonard said. "You ready to go, James?"

"No," I said. "Can't you see we're playing?"

"We need to get ready for the movie," Mom said. "The show starts in half an hour."

"Come with us," Jim told me.

"Yeah," Barry said. "You'll like it. It's got aliens and stuff."

"What about it, Leonard?" I asked my former teacher. "It's got aliens and stuff."

"Why not," he said.

A half hour later we were all at the old Cameo Theatre watching the opening credits to *Close Encounters*. Leonard really seemed to enjoy spending time with the children. It was almost dark when we all walked back out to the parking lot.

Jim, Jaime, Larry, and my brothers followed Leonard and me out to the El Camino. I opened the passenger door, dropped into the seat, and slammed the door behind me. Leonard slipped in behind the steering wheel and started to close his door.

"Thanks for the rocket," Jim said. "And the comic books."

"You're welcome, Jim," Leonard said. "Hope you enjoy it for years to come." He slammed his door and started the engine. We turned the El Camino around and started down the driveway.

My younger counterpart, friends, and brothers were waving behind us.

"Where to now?" Leonard asked.

Chapter 8: Full Circle

Jim was home watching television by himself when the phone rang. His parents had gone to the grocery store. His brothers were upstairs playing with an electric football game. Jim picked up the phone.

"Hello."

"Jim!" It was Jaime's voice on the line. She sounded excited. "Jim you've got to come down to Miracle Mountain Park there was a UFO and something came out of it and crashed on Ghost Mountain and the police are all going up there and you've got to come see it!"

Jim hung up about two minutes later. He wondered what had really happened. If aliens had really landed outside of town, he'd get his folks to drive him up there as soon as they got home. He hated to disappoint Jaime. She'd really sounded dejected when she hung up.

The sun was down and only the faintest tinge of red still clung to the horizon. A little girl pedaled a rickety boy's bike up a hill. The thin cotton shirt she wore wasn't much of a shield against the cool, night wind that blew down over the mountains. She was starting to notice that. But it was too late to go back now.

I was standing in tall grass in the clearing beside the wax museum. Flashing lights from police vehicles gave me the feeling of being in some weird, outdoor disco. The grounds were choked with police cars and the vehicles of local passers-by. The helicopter, its propeller twisted and ruined, lay at an angle in a heap of bushes. Vines clung to the propeller and the skids. The blades had topped several trees on the way down. The police and sheriff's men were trying to clear the area of curious townspeople. Two or three voices echoed weirdly through bullhorns. I recognized Billy Neeson's voice by the slurred speech and bad grammar. Any opportunity he had to grandstand and give orders was too much temptation to refuse. People were slowly returning to their vehicles. The gaggle of seventies vehicles reminded me of an antique car show. Dr. Tarkington was there in his Hawaiian shirt. Larry, Keith Anderson and the rest of the helicopter's passengers were standing by the rear door of an ambulance surrounded by a knot of policemen and paramedics. Tension seemed to be building. Then I heard the cries of confusion.

"Get back!" Keith Anderson yelled. "I don't want to hurt anybody, but I've got to have some answers."

He had snatched a gun from one of the stunned policemen and was pointing it with a badly trembling right hand.

"Now, simmer down, son," Sheriff McNeal said. "Nobody's gonna hurt ya."

"Put the gun down, Keith," Tarkington said. "This isn't going to solve anything."

My brain kicked into slow motion. I felt like I was underwater, like I was standing outside of my body watching everything take place. Anderson bolted and ran. His face had become the nightmare-stricken face of a young boy. He was only nineteen years old, but he seemed even younger. I saw one of the policemen fire a shot over his head. The shot echoed like a thunderclap.

"No!" Tarkington cried.

"Don't shoot him!" the sheriff was shouting.

"Stop!" I heard voices yell.

"Stop!"

"Surrender!"

" . . . won't be hurt!"

" . . . won't hurt you!"

Several of the others started chasing him. Anderson turned and fired over their heads. They ducked behind cars. One of them fired at him, nicked his side. His shirt darkened with blood.

"NO!" Tarkington cried again. He tackled the man with the gun.

Anderson looked down at his shirt, touched it with his empty hand. A look of mortal terror filled his face. Tears ran down his face. My throat went dry. I felt my heart pounding in my ears.

Anderson slammed into me, knocked me off my feet.

"Stop!" I yelled. "Stop!"

Anderson leaped onto my bike and stomped the foot pedal. Again. Again. He cried out in rage and stomped it again. The police were gaining on him.

"Anderson!" I yelled. I grabbed him by his shoulders. He had dropped the gun.

"Anderson," I yelled. "Stop it! KEITH!" He froze as he realized I had called him by his name.

"I'm a friend of Dr. Tarkington's," I said.

"Tark?" he repeated, half comprehending.

"I came back from the future to keep you from getting yourself killed. You're going to be all right. Everything's going to be all right." He took a deep breath, wiped his face. He looked down at the stain on his shirt. "It's just a nick," I told him. "You'll be all right."

The police had surrounded us by that time.

"Go with them," I said. "They'll take you to a doctor. I'll see you on the other side."

"Thanks, man," he said.

"Go easy on him," I told the cops. "He's just scared."

They looked at me strangely.

"*Who does he think he is?*" they asked with their eyes. Anderson left with them.

I had done it! Keith Anderson was alive. Jaime wasn't going to die. I had broken the cycle. Thank God, I had broken the cycle.

My hands were trembling when I reconnected my sparkplug wire. I pulled a helmet on, and kick-started my bike. I passed by the ambulance and the crowd of police officers and paramedics as I was leaving. Between the backs of two state troopers, I saw Dr. Tarkington and Larry standing there in cuffs. The helmet I was wearing covered my face, but I saw Larry frown and wondered if he had recognized me anyway. I gave him a quick "thumbs up" sign and left the scene before the police got too curious. I drove around a large rock and a bank of trees. Leonard was standing beside his truck holding up a brightly painted banner.

"ANDERSON! SURRENDER! IT'S OK!"

He stepped out into the road waving it desperately.

"It's okay," I said stopping. I raised the visor of my helmet. "It's me. We did it. We managed to stop him."

"Thank the Lord!" he said. He breathed a sigh of relief. "Thank God."

"At the last minute I realized something," I told him, "something that shook me to the core."

"What's that?" he asked.

"I've been here before," I told him.

"Come again?"

"It's hard to explain," I told him. "Ever since Tarkington's bunch made the first accidental trip through time, we've been caught in a loop. We've been repeating the accident over and over again, but it's a little different each time."

"And every time you go through, you think it's the first time?"

"Right. In the last cycle, the one before this one, another version of me came back here to save the Jaime, and failed. In that cycle, Anderson stole my--his bike and caused the accident. Jaime died because of me."

"How do you know that?"

"Two things," I said. "When I was visiting my parents, I saw a home movie of my birthday party."

"The party from today?"

"Yes," I said. "I was in the movie. It was only a glimpse, but it was me. I was there. What's more, I remembered meeting myself when I was twelve."

"How do you know about the bike?" he asked.

"When I got to the scene of the accident," I told him, "I started to get off the bike. That's when I looked down and saw the turn indicator lights. They were yellow and molded into the shapes of arrows. I found one of them at the scene of the accident when I was twelve. Same shape and color. I knew my bike would be involved in that accident, so I disconnected the sparkplug wire before Anderson could get there."

"So he couldn't get the bike to start," Leonard said. "Now Anderson and Jaime are still alive. Brilliant."

"More like lucky," I said.

"Or blessed from behind the scenes," he said. "Who knows?"

I pulled my bike up beside the truck. A small, vulnerable-looking figure was seated inside. I opened the door.

"Hey, good lookin'," I said. "How ya doin'?"

Jaime spun around and wrapped her arms around my neck. She squeezed hard. I clung to her living, breathing body as if I had just ripped her from the Reaper's cold, bony hands. I kissed her hair and told her how everything was going to be all right, how I would take care of her and not let anything happen to her. Finally we separated.

"I'll see you at Jim's parents' house," I said.

"See ya, Jim," she said. Then she smiled one of those enchanting smiles of hers. It didn't occur to me until later that she had called me *Jim*, not *Mr. James*.

Two minutes later we were roaring back through town. I felt like I was giving Leonard a police escort. We came up behind my parents as they were coming back from the grocery store. I passed them, waving as I went around them. I stayed just ahead of them and pulled into the yard to wait. Jim came outside to see what was happening. Jaime got out of Leonard's El Camino, ran up to him, and hugged him hard. Jim looked both pleased and embarrassed.

We all went inside. Mom called Lisa Mitchell and invited her to come over and talk. She'd just found Jaime's note about running away and had just delivered a tearful call to an overwhelmed police department. She came to the door about five minutes later. I thought she might throw a cussing, screaming fit and haul Jaime out to the car, but she was pretty subdued. She hugged her daughter, cried a little, and settled in to tell her story.

The daughter of an alcoholic mechanic, Lisa had married the manager of a restaurant where she had worked as a waitress. The man was divorced, and he had a son, but he had seemed to be a caring family man. He was also, it turned out, an alcoholic.

For a time, the girl had dreamed of a day when he would love her enough to leave the wild life alone for good. She had given him a baby daughter, had been the best wife she knew how to be, and the best mother to his son.

One night during a drunken rage, he had threatened to kill not only Lisa, but also her daughter who was asleep in the next room. In a panic, Lisa had taken her daughter and everything she could carry, had packed it into her ancient Rambler, had left Donnie Mitchell once and for all.

With no education beyond high school, she had secured a job at a convenience store and was barely managing to keep the bills paid. Food stamps had helped.

The threats against her own life and that of her daughter—and the guilt and concern for the stepson she had left behind--had haunted Lisa in her dreams. Many were the nights she had dreamed of waking up and finding that Jaime had been taken from her. And every time her fun-loving and oh-so-carefree daughter had disappeared on another of her adventures, Lisa had panicked.

It was 3:00 A.M. before the conversation finally wound down.

"It's so late," my mom said. "Why don't we just bed you and Jaime down here for the night? That couch in the den makes out into a bed."

Lisa and my parents peeled Jaime and me--the twelve-year-old me--off of the couch where we had been sleeping. Jim was sent up to his room. He shuffled up the stairs on zombie-like automatic pilot. Lisa propped Jaime up until Mom threw some sheets onto the hide-a-bed. Then she laid her out on the mattress and tucked her in. I kissed her on the cheek.

"I've got to go," I said.

Leonard and I started to leave.

"Thanks so much for taking care of Jaime," Lisa told both of us. "I was trying to do it alone. Sometimes you just can't." She hugged us each in turn.

Leonard and I started for the El Camino.

"I think your mother wants to tell you something," Leonard said. He pointed back at the house with his thumb.

"What?" I asked. My mother?

Mom was standing on the porch. She motioned for me.

"Wait here for a minute," I told Leonard. I walked back to the porch.

"Jim," she said.

"Yes, ma'am," I said. "What is it?"

"You are Jim, aren't you?" she asked. That's when I noticed she had called me "Jim" instead of "James."

I tried to think of a convincing half-truth, but none would come. I don't guess it really mattered since she already knew anyway.

"Yes," I said. I laughed and grinned sheepishly. "Yeah, it's me."

"I knew you looked familiar when I saw you at the birthday party," she said. "When we were talking in the house, it hit me who you were. I couldn't really believe it, but there were things about you, even the way you walked."

"Oh, man," I said. "Not the walk again. What's so unusual about my walk?"

"Finding Jaime tonight wasn't a coincidence, was it?"

"No," I said. "No, it wasn't."

"This is why you came back? To help Jaime?"

"To save her life," I said. "In the childhood I remember, Jaime died on the night of my twelfth birthday."

She put her hand to her mouth and nodded.

"Docs Dad know too?" I asked. "Who I am, I mean?"

"He caught the resemblance," she said. "Just like I did. But he's too practical to even think about you really being Jim."

"I'd better go now," I said. "I'll see you in a few years."

"Thanks for coming," Mom said. She hugged me. "Thanks for being the man we raised you to be."

"What if I'm not?" I laughed, hugging her back.

"You can't fool me," she said.

"I never could," I told her. We smiled at each other.

I walked back to the truck. Leonard and I rode back to the Delaney house without saying more than two words. Both of us were exhausted. I barely even remember getting into bed that night. I just know I slept well.

Chapter 9: Departure

I was back in the ninth grade. I accepted this without question. I came out of the principal's office. Jaime was waiting there for me. She was about fourteen, stylishly dressed, and still not much over five feet tall. Her hair was a long pile of dark ringlets.

"I'm so proud of you for standing up to him."

"I got suspended, Jaime," I said miserably, "and I'm the head of the youth council at church. I'll probably get kicked off."

"That was great," Jaime said. "I'll never forget the look on his face when you knocked those mirrored shades off, and he fell over the trash can." *She punched the air a couple of times.* *"Then you bloodied his nose. It was great! I'm so proud of you!"* *She squeezed up against my side. I couldn't keep from smiling.*

"You have no idea how long I've wanted to do that," I admitted. "It's probably a sin."

"God will forgive you," Jaime said. "Don't know if Goose ever will."

"Hmm," I said. "I just wonder who really threw that Coke on him."

Jaime smiled sweetly and shrugged.

I woke up. It took me an instant to realize where—and when—I was. This was Leonard Delaney's guest room in 1977. My dream of Jaime as a high school student had seemed so vivid, so real. It was like something that really might have happened. It seemed more likely, in fact, than time travel. I looked at the clock. It was nearly noon. A dark realization gripped my heart. This was the day I was to leave, to return to my own time. I had wanted the day to be a cheerful and normal day, a golden summer day like the others I had spent. The day was fine, but I wasn't. I was leaving.

Leonard was preparing lunch when I walked into the kitchen. He'd cooked up some macaroni and cheese and some pork 'n' beans. He was stirring the pots when I came in.

"How's this for lunch?" he asked.

"Fine," I said. "Bachelor gourmet."

He passed me a plate. I served myself out of pots he'd left on the stove. He poured us both glasses of iced tea.

I sat down at the table. Leonard said grace the way he always did, and we started eating.

"Preacher just called to make sure I hadn't fallen down in the bathtub or anything," he said, amused.

"Oh," I said. "It is Sunday morning, isn't it?"

"No," he said. "It's Sunday afternoon."

"I hope you didn't miss church because of me," I said.

"Are you kidding?" he said. "I couldn't have dragged these old bones out of bed this morning if my eternal destiny had depended on it."

We didn't talk much after that. We both knew what this day meant.

After lunch, I loaded everything I had brought with me into my backpack. Leonard helped me lift my motorcycle into the back of his truck. I looked over the guest room for the last time.

"Ready to go?" he asked.

"Ready as I'll ever be," I said.

As we rolled back through Miracle Springs, I took a long look at things like the Tastee Freeze, the movie marquee, and a baseball field that was now the parking lot of a McDonald's. I took it all in one last time.

Before we left town, I asked Leonard to pull in at the parking lot of the post office. I pulled two envelopes out of the backpack I was carrying on my lap.

"What's this?" Leonard asked.

"I'm mailing CDs to both Colonel Holden and to Dr. Tarkington, the scientist who will discover the anomalies," I told him. "They won't be able to read them until they need to. I also gave one to my younger self and told him to open it on his twenty-fifth birthday. This time, we're going to make sure the changes in history stay put."

I opened the door, walked over to the "Out of Town" box, and dropped the envelope in. I walked back to the truck and climbed into the truck and slammed the passenger side door.

We rolled out of town without saying much as we passed between cliffs left when the road crews had blasted through mountains. We rode up a hill through the forest, around some hairpin curves, past Welcome Church, past the ditch Billy Neeson had driven his car into, and down to the oil road from which I'd first entered 1977.

The rusty gate to the road was closed, chained, and padlocked. We would have to walk.

I climbed up into the bed of the El Camino, stood my bike up onto its tires, and dropped it off the back, one tire at a time. Leonard stood on the ground and helped me lower it.

I pushed the bike under the gate.

We walked a little over a hundred yards together to a plateau surrounded on three sides by sharp drops into the forest and on one side by a tall cliff. Oil well equipment--tanks and a grasshopper pump--stood beside a pit filled with black slime.

Then I heard the thumping of helicopter blades.

"There it is," I said, pointing up.

The sun was glinting off something. A metal insect dropped from the sky and touched down on the plateau.

"I guess this is it," I said. I looked back at Leonard Delaney knowing this was the last time I would ever see him alive. I started to shake hands with him, but we ended up hugging each other.

"You take care now," he finally said, his voice hoarse. "It's not going to be the same around here without you. You brought a sense of wonder back into my life that I never thought I'd feel again."

"I'm glad I got a chance to see you again," I said. "Take care of Jaime for me." The request seemed hollow since he would only have six months to live.

"You've got it," he smiled, clapped me on both shoulders. "You've got it!"

"Mr. Delaney," I heard a familiar voice say. "It's good to see you again."

Larry Christopher--the adult Larry Christopher--walked up to Mr. Delaney and extended a hand.

"Larry?" Mr. Delaney smiled. "Well, how are you?"

Taking a deep breath and turning away from them, I pushed my bike to the skid and strapped it in place. Larry and I said our last hasty goodbyes and climbed into the waiting chopper.

"How was your trip?" Colonel Holden asked.

"Great," I said. "Best time of my life."

"Good," he said. That was when I noticed a young man standing beside him.

"Anderson?"

He smiled.

"It's nice to meet you," he said. "Thanks for saving my life." I shook his hand and remembered the newspaper clipping on Tarkington's desk. That was only a memory now.

I strapped in.

"Let's rock," Jefferson, the co-pilot, said. The chopper lifted off. Leonard sat in the clearing waving to us as we flew away. I felt a lump form in my throat as I watched him shrink away to a tiny dot and vanish from sight. I looked over at Larry. There were tears on his face.

A circular cloud hung over Ghost Mountain. In broad daylight, few would have even noticed it. Larry aimed for the center and shot us into it. Suddenly it was night and we were flying beneath the light of a big full moon. The cloudy portal glowed behind us for nearly a minute before dissipating into the cool night air.

"We're baaaaaack!" Jefferson, the co-pilot, said.

Chapter 10: Homecoming

They flew me to Braxton Air Force Base for a debriefing. I spent nearly a week there being interviewed about the details of my trip and about my personal life and memories. Everything I said was taken down with extreme care. My memories were like two versions of a movie script that had been thrown together without any editing. Every day I seemed to remember new things. The altered memories seemed to resurface in random bursts. The memories of my old life grew less vivid, but I still had them. The psychiatrists watched all of this with extreme interest. No one had ever done an in-depth study of the effects of time travel on memory. As Holden had explained to me before the trip back, no one knew what effect altering—or restoring—my past would have on my mind.

Finally, at the end of seven days, I was taken to a counseling room with comfortable chairs and a kitchenette. Colonel Holden was waiting for me. He dismissed the orderlies who had brought me and invited me to sit down. He had been up pacing around. Finally he sighed and sat down beside me.

"That takes care of the interviews," he said. "We're about to release you. The cover story is that you suffered a blow to the head during an expedition. You lost your memory, but your brain is recovering nicely." He stopped, got up. "Would you like some coffee, James?"

"Sure," I said. "Why not?" He went to the door.

"Could you bring us some coffee please?" he said to someone out in the hall.

A moment later a young woman in a bright-colored scrub suit came in with a cup of coffee. Her dark hair was pulled into a French braid. She looked familiar.

"Do you have any other questions?" Holden asked.

"A ton of them," I said. "I don't know where to begin." I took a swallow of the coffee. The taste was familiar, strangely familiar.

"Wait a minute," I said. Then I looked at the coffee. "Chocolate macadamia nut? How did you know about that?"

The girl in scrubs was walking out the door. Suddenly I knew.

"Jaime?"

She froze for a moment, then turned. She was smiling, but her eyes were bright with tears.

"My absent-minded genius," she said. "I'm glad you still remember me."

I stumbled to my feet. We stood facing each other.

"You're so beautiful," I told her.

"I know," she said. "Thanks for noticing."

I hugged her, held her tight.

"You're not much taller than you were then," I told her.

"Maybe not," she said. "But that doesn't mean I haven't changed."

She grabbed me and kissed me. I was breathless when she finally let me go.

"Grown-up Jaime is going to take some getting used to," I said. She laughed. It was the same girlish giggle I'd heard so many times from the younger Jaime.

"I'll give you two some time together," Holden said.

"I don't know about that," I told him. "She looks dangerous."

He smiled and stepped outside.

"So you just got back from 1977?" Jaime asked. She sat down on the table.

"Yeah," I said. "Only a week ago, I was with you, Leonard Delaney, and my folks back in Miracle Springs."

"You don't know how long I've wanted to talk to you about all of this," she said. "But I couldn't."

"You knew who I was?" I asked.

"It wasn't hard to figure out," she said. "You don't look that different . . . and you even had the same walk."

"What is it about my walk?" I asked her. She smiled and shrugged.

"I wish the trip through time hadn't scrambled up your memories, Jim, but it's so good to finally be able to talk to you about all of this. I grew up knowing the truth, but there were times I wondered if I was crazy to believe it." She stopped. "After we get out of here, let's go home."

"Home?" I said.

"Yeah," she said. "Didn't he tell you we were married?"

"No," I said. "How long?"

"Five years," she said.

"Wow. Do we have any kids?"

"Not yet."

"Where do we live?"

"Miracle Springs. We just moved back."

* * *

That night we were sitting on the couch together in our den. Jaime had her bare feet pulled up beside me and there was a photo album, a stack of VHS tapes, and a bowl of popcorn on the table in front of us. Jaime had a VCR remote in her hand. She was narrating her way through a video of our wedding. I was both surprised and relieved to see some of my old college friends there among the guests. The church was familiar to me. I had attended Temple Baptist Church as a college student in my "other life." What was I supposed to call that life exactly?

I saw myself standing at the front of the room in a black tuxedo. Larry, my brothers, and some of my college friends were there with me. Jaime's mother and brother were seated beside my parents on the front row. The guests rose and the camera panned to the back of the church. Jaime appeared there. Her dress was long and covered with seed pearls. There were flowers in her hair. Walking beside her was an elderly white-haired man. I gasped and leaped to my feet.

* * *

It was almost midnight. Jaime and I were sitting in a hot tub looking out on a field and the mountains beyond it. I could see the lights of my parents' house up the hill and across a pasture. As Jaime and I sat there under the stars, we could hear the chirping of crickets. The grass had just been cut. It was fresh-smelling and wet with dew. Jaime was squeezed up against my side in a bathing suit.

The screen door opened, and we heard the rattling of ice cubes in glasses. Leonard Delaney stepped out carrying a tray full of drinking glasses. He was grayer and frailer than when I'd seen him last, but he still had that same gleam of intelligence and mischief in his eyes.

"I see you like the improvements I've made to the place," he said.

"It's great," Jaime said. "Perfect."

He set the tray down on a picnic table.

"Good for arthritis, too," he said. "But you wouldn't know anything about that yet."

"You just got a jacuzzi so girls would come to see you," I told him.

"Works too," he said, smiling. "I got a Coke for you and a root beer for Miss Jaime." He handed us the glasses.

"I can't believe you're really here," I told him. We'd already gotten past the teary-eyed stage, but I was still overwhelmed by the idea of seeing Leonard Delaney alive and living next door to my parents in 1997. I knew he couldn't live forever, and that I'd eventually lose him again, but I had him back for now.

"I can't believe I used to be dead," he shrugged. "You say I died of a heart attack back in fall of 1977?"

"Yeah," I said. "In November. I'm still trying to figure out what I could have done that changed history."

"You asked me to take care of Jaime," he said. "Right before you left, you asked me to take care of her. Do you remember that?"

"Yes," I said. "Like it was yesterday—or last week, anyway." They smiled.

"Having somebody to love, somebody who needs you," he stopped, shook his head. "That makes all the difference, James. All the difference in the world."

He sat down beside the hot tub and gazed up at the stars. It was nearly two in the morning when we went in and went to bed.

THE SIGN OF THE SWORD
By Timothy D. Wise

On an icy November night, four high school students and their teacher take a carriage ride through a foggy forest and find themselves in another world. Chased through the forest by silver-eyed cyborgs, attacked by a werewolf, and rescued by a ragged stranger who claims to be the heir to King Arthur's throne, the travelers find that their only chance to return home lies in restoring the kingdom of Camelot on an alien world.

ISBN: 0-9725549-5-5
$12.95
216 pages

THRILLS AND CHILLS FOR GROWN-UP READERS!

CHUNCHUBA
By K. Michael Casey

Less than 500 years ago, the Biloxi Indian tribe vanished without a trace. The mystery of their disappearance has never been completely explained. Now a brooding presence has returned to the dark waters of coastal Mississippi and people are disappearing again. Scientist Nathan Young and his estranged wife Kat are drawn into the mystery by Kat's Native American heritage and a secret tragedy that hangs over her past. Doctor John, a terrifying voodoo priest seeks to control the Chinchuba's power. Kevin Croix, an unorthodox street evangelist is drawn by prophecy to stand against it. Can the Chinchuba be beaten back or are those in its path doomed to share the fate of the Biloxi tribe?

ISBN: 0-9725549-6-3
$14.95
276 pages